MW01154697

BITTER BABY MAMA'S CLUB

A novel by Lady Lissa & Shay Renee

Copyright © 2018 Lady Lissa & Shay Renee
Published by Unique Pen Publications, LLC
All rights reserved. No part of this book may be reproduced in any form without written consent of the publisher, except brief quotes used in reviews.
This is a work of fiction. Any references or similarities to actual events, real people, living or dead, or to real locals are intended to give the novel a sense of reality. Any similarity in other names, characters, places, and incidents are entirely coincidental.

PROLOGUE

Cedrica

"Marcus, I don't give a fuck about how you feel about me! At the end of the day, you ain't gotta do shit for me! Just take care of your damn child!" I yelled as I tightly held onto the pink Mickey Mouse infant carrier.

I looked down at the beautiful baby girl who was sound asleep. She looked so innocent and angelic in her yellow cotton onesie with the matching mittens. Jakayla was my rainbow baby, and unfortunately her father's biggest regret. Most men were elated once they found out they had a daughter, but not Marcus. His reaction was the complete opposite, and I was beyond fed up with his shit.

"Drica, you know damn well I ain't got a problem taking care of what's mine. But…"

"But what? She's yours and you know it! Ever since this hoe got back in the picture all you ever do is deny her! But all before you was ready to be a father!" I shouted as I looked at the female standing beside him.

She laughed and shook her head.

"First of all bitch, I BEEN in the picture and I'm tired of you fucking speaking on my name! What this nigga do or don't do ain't got shit to do with me! And second of all, bitch, you the one who chose to wait five months after he left your dumb ass to speak up about being pregnant! That's why you're in the situation you're in now! Had you opened your mouth sooner, maybe he'd take the little bastard being his into consideration!"

"Keisha shut the fuck up! How the hell did I wait five months? You been knowing what time it was since you busted up at the cabin. When it comes down to our child, you ain't got shit to do with it! Matter of fact, why are you even here?!"

"Because, I'm his wife, bitch! That's why!"

I squinted my eyes and turned to Marcus. Now, I wasn't going to lie and say that I had this fairytale notion that the two of us would be together after I had this baby, but I certainly didn't think he'd marry the bitch that had been giving me hell the past few months.

"Your wife? So, you really married this hoe?"

"Yes, he did! When you was in the hospital pushing out your future, I was saying I do to mine!"

"Wow!" I yelled as I stared at Marcus. "So that's why you couldn't come to the hospital, Marcus? That's why you couldn't be there for the birth of our daughter? Huh? That's why you weren't responding to my texts and calls?! You were actually somewhere marrying HER!! How could you?"

"Man look, all this shit is irrelevant. You out here tryna put this kid on me and she ain't got shit for me."

"What the fuck is that supposed to mean?"

"All my kids look like me Drica. Same eyes, same nose, same ears, and they all got the same last name. She ain't got none of that shit. Nothing."

I placed the infant seat on the ground beside me, then locked my apartment door and faced him.

"See, that's what's wrong with you niggas these days!" I shouted as I placed my keys in the black Moschino Baby Teddy Bear

Diaper Bag that hung off of my shoulder. "Y'all always expect the baby to come out looking like y'all in order for y'all to claim it! Newsflash nigga, she don't have to have your eyes, or your nose, or your damn last name to be your blood! And how the fuck was she gonna get your last name anyway when you skipped coming to the hospital to go and give it to that bitch? The whole time we were together you begged me to have a baby for you, and now that she's here you're basically telling me that you don't want shit to do with her!"

"Bitch, how about you just do a DNA test so all this shit can be resolved!" Keisha shouted. "You standing up here doing all this hooping and hollering, but don't wanna get a fucking test done! If it's his then you shouldn't have shit to worry about!"

"Marcus, I'm telling you now, get your hoe! Please, get your hoe!"

"Nah, she right. I been telling you I wanted a DNA test. So until you do it, it's nothing."

"It's nothing?! Nigga you act like I was just out there tricking or something!"

"I don't know what the fuck you was doing once I left."

"It doesn't matter what I was doing before you left because you been knowing I was pregnant. Instead of walking around denying her, you need to stop letting this motherfucker control you and man the fuck up!"

"Bitch you got one more time to disrespect me," Keisha said as she took off her earrings.

"Or what? What the fuck you gonna do? I wish you would put your fucking hands on me while I got my child in my presence!"

"Girl don't nobody give a fuck about you or your child! I'll whip her ass too!"

"Keisha, go back to the truck!" Marcus shouted before I could reply.

"Fuck no! I ain't going nowhere! If she would've gotten the abortion like you told her to, none of this shit would be going on!"

"Abortion?" I asked confusingly.

"Yea bitch! You heard me!"

"Keisha!" Marcus shouted again. "Go to the fucking truck my nigga!"

She sucked her teeth and rolled her eyes, then turned around and began walking down the stairs. When she got to the bottom, she stopped and looked up at me.

"COUNT YOUR DAYS BITCH! BECAUSE I WILL SEE YOUR ASS AGAIN REAL SOON!"

"Girl fuck you! See your way into somebody's clinic hoe and quit worrying about me and mine!"

"FIND YOUR BABY DADDY BITCH AND STOP STALKING MY HUSBAND! YOU WAS NEVER NOTHING BUT A SLIDE!"

"Yea, a slide that slid out a baby for him!" I clapped back.

"Bitch you sound just as stupid as you look!"

"KEISHA! CHILL THE FUCK OUT AND GO ON MAN!" Marcus yelled.

She chucked up the deuces and pulled out her phone, then walked away. I looked at Marcus and shook my head.

"You're really a sad person, you know that?"

"Look Drica, I ain't got time to stand here and argue with you about some shit we already discussed. I said what I had to say, and that's that. Whenever you decide you're ready to do the test, holla at me. But when the results come back, you gon' see that I've been right all along."

"Right about what? About being a fucking deadbeat? Cuz everything else that's coming out of your mouth is bullshit! Like, you're really putting a fucking clown before your child!"

"Call it what you want," he chuckled. "But at the end of the day it is what it is. Keisha ain't making me do shit, so stop it. I just ain't finna take care of no baby that ain't mine, so if you thought that's how shit was gonna go down, you got the wrong nigga love."

"You know what?" I sighed. "You're right! At this point, what you're saying doesn't even matter, cuz everybody already knows the truth! Everybody saying…"

"Man, listen, I honestly don't give a fuck about what you or anybody saying, and that includes your fucking family! Cuz I know they're the ones behind all this shit!"

"My family ain't got shit to do with this, so don't even go there!"

"Man, get the fuck out of here with that bullshit! You know just like I know your family got everything to do with this! They stay in your fucking business, which is why shit between us went downhill in the first place!"

"Boy, please! Shit went downhill because of you and your hoes, so don't try to put none of that on my damn family! Like I said, this ain't got shit to do with nobody but me and you!"

"You knew what it was before you bent over, so don't pull that card! And why the fuck you standing here mentioning shit about 'everybody' else if it's between us? Just tell the truth! You saw a baby as a way to get paid! If all you wanted was money my nigga you could've been asked for that!"

"This ain't about no fucking money!" I shouted.

"So what the fuck is it about then Drica? Cuz it seems like you ain't after shit but a check!"

"You know what Marcus," I sighed. "You're right! I am after a check, a reality check for your ass! It's time you realize that you can't just go through life dodging your responsibilities and living as if they do not exist!"

"What the fuck are you talking about?" He asked with a confused look on his face. "You tryna be on some Dr. Phil shit?"

I swallowed hard and took a step back.

"Not at all! I'm filing for child support!"

"You doing what?"

"You heard me! I said I'm filing for child support! I tried to keep things cordial and give you a chance to do right, but we can't seem to come to an agreement on our own without your rat getting involved! You wanna play like you don't know Jakayla is yours and deny her, so we can just kill two birds with one stone and get it all over with through the courts!"

"Drica, what did you just say?"

"Uh, did I stutter? I already repeated it twice when I know you heard me the first damn time," I said. I was tired of playing this game with him. If he wanted to let that hoodrat dictate his relationship with his daughter, then so be it. We could get the courts to remedy that shit real quick.

"Are you fuckin' serious right now, bruh?"

"DEAD ASS!" I replied as I nodded my head. "I'm tired of arguing with you, and I'm tired of you denying OUR child! This way will be much easier for all of us!"

"Easier for us? How the fuck is that supposed to be easier?" He fumed.

"Well, it's gon' be easier for me. How 'bout that?"

"Drica you really fucked up for that shit!" Marcus replied as he shot me a sinister look.

I placed my hand on my hip and sighed, then turned around and picked up the baby carrier.

"I tried being civil with you, but unfortunately that didn't work! I'm all out of options Marcus! You made your bed on more than one occasion! Now it's time for you to lie in it the same way you lied WITH and TO me! I'm done talking! Oh, and tell your wife I'll see her ass in court too!"

"For what?!"

"Since you can't seem to keep the bitch away from me, I'm filing charges for harassment!"

With that, I tossed my hair over my shoulders and twisted my hips all the way down the stairs. I was tired of dealing with this bullshit from my baby daddy. If I had any doubts about my child being his, I would have spoken up a long time ago instead of just trying to pin her on him. But I never was the type to sleep around, so I knew for a fact that Marcus was my baby's daddy. All I was trying to do was give him the opportunity to be part of his daughter's life, but since he wanted to play games, two could do that shit.

Let the games begin...

CHAPTER ONE

London

If somebody would've told me two weeks ago that I'd be sitting in a clinic with a nurse telling me that I tested positive for pregnancy, I would've offered them a fight. I wasn't trying to have any more kids. I already had two girls by two different deadbeat daddies, so the last thing I needed was to have another kid by another deadbeat. I should've known when I missed my period that I was pregnant, but my period had always been irregular. Why would I rush to get a pregnancy test when I had an irregular cycle?

"Come again," I said to the nurse.

"I said that you're pregnant," she repeated.

"That can't be. Can we take another test please?"

"Another test isn't necessary. This test is very accurate. I can assure you that you are having a baby."

"Oh my God! Are you serious?"

"Yes…"

I jumped up and rushed toward the door. "Wait! Don't you want to know when you're due?" The nurse asked as she stood there looking at me like I was a two headed monster.

I didn't bother answering as I rushed through the lobby and out the door. I headed to the bus stop and sat there waiting for the next bus to come. I was stunned by the news that she gave me. That was something I didn't expect to hear at all. I wished she had told me that I had an STD instead of telling me that I was having another baby.

Shyanna was two and Gracie was three, now I was having another kid. Oh, hell no!

I pulled out my phone and looked up the number to the women's clinic. "Jacksonville Women's Clinic, how may I help you?"

"I was just calling for some information please," I said in a shaky voice. I tried to steady my tone, but I couldn't. The truth was I was nervous about calling them. Hell, I was nervous about being pregnant again. I struggled to take care of my two children by myself because their fathers wouldn't help me out.

Shyanna's sperm donor had been avoiding the subpoena for child support court for about two months now. I knew he still lived with his aunt, but whenever they went to serve him with the court papers, he wouldn't open the door. And Gracie's sperm donor was doing three to ten in county jail. Now, I was having a baby by Shane… there was no way I was having this baby.

"Ma'am…" I had totally forgotten that I had the woman from the clinic on the phone.

"Yes, I'm sorry, what?"

"You said you needed some information. What kind of information do you need?"

"Yes, if I wanted to terminate a pregnancy, how much would it cost?"

"Well, that depends on how far along you are. Do you know how many months you are?"

"No."

"I just need to know how far along you are in order to give you a price. The cost could range from $450 to $1500."

"That much?!" I asked. I was shocked that an abortion would be so expensive.

"Yes. Would you like to make an appointment?"

"Not at this time, thank you." I quickly ended the call because I had nothing else to say. How the hell could I afford that much money to have an abortion? Dammit! I could kick myself for that shit. How could I let that happen again?

I couldn't believe that I was pregnant again. I had worked so hard to get myself fine again after giving birth to Gracie two years ago. Because I was only 5'6", I couldn't afford to be too heavy. When I was pregnant with Gracie, I gained a whole 24 pounds. I worked like a damn slave to lose those 24 pounds too. Now, I was 135 pounds with thick thighs and a fat ass. I loved to get my hair done, but couldn't always afford it, so sometimes my weave lasted a little longer than it should have. Hey, I was a single mom, so I couldn't get my hair done every month like some of the other bitches. But I still looked good with my creamy brown skin, hazel colored eyes and pouty lips which I inherited from my mom. I was a very attractive chick, so I didn't know why I always found niggas who didn't give a fuck about me or our kids.

I called Shane because I needed to talk to him ASAP. He didn't answer the first time, so I called back. "What dude, damn?" He answered the second time.

"Why are you coming at me like that?" I asked. The fact that I had just found out I was pregnant already had me feeling some kind of way. Hearing him answer the phone like that when he knew it was me quickly incinerated what little happiness I had left.

"I got shit going on right now, so what the hell you want London?"

"Are you coming by tonight?" I asked.

"I'on know, why?"

"I need you to roll through later."

"What for? I mean, you already got me on the phone, so you might as well say what you called to say," he said.

"Nah, I'll wait. You just need to roll through."

"I ain't making no promises to do that. Look, I gotta go," he said and hung the phone up before I had a chance to answer.

I hated that I had gotten involved with him, especially since I had been forewarned not to. What the hell was I thinking? Oh yea, I was thinking that I was a grown ass bitch and I could do whatever the hell I wanted to do. Now that I had gotten pregnant, I wished I had listened to those warnings. I sat at the bus stop as tears rained down my face. I didn't know what I was going to do now. I was already on Section 8 receiving rental assistance and getting food stamps to buy groceries. But what was I going to do with a new baby?

My youngest had just graduated to panties, and now I had to revert back to diapers. How was I gonna afford all those diapers with my small salary from the dollar store. Ugh! I hated my life in that moment and wished that I could just fall into a hole and die.

◆ ◆ ◆

I had finally got to sleep after what seemed like hours of trying. My mind was so full and kept going back to the fact that I was pregnant. Shane hadn't even come by the way I had hoped so I could break the news to him. It was little shit like that which made me realize what a mistake I had made with him. He already had three baby mamas and four kids that he didn't take care of.

Well, that isn't completely true. He took care of one of his kids, but that was because he was still sleeping with that baby's mama. I didn't want to be a baby mama, but that was how shit turned out in my life. Anyway, I had finally gotten comfortable enough to fall asleep when I felt some hands creeping up my thighs to remove my panties. I didn't even panic because I wasn't surprised that Shane had shown up in the middle of the night. He wanted to make sure we didn't have anything to speak about by the time he came through.

I lifted my butt so he could pull my panties off, as he slid between my legs and inserted his dick inside me. I wanted to stop him because we really needed to talk, but how could I? My pussy was feeling so good as it throbbed against his dick. I just spread my legs wider as he pummeled inside me. The sensations had my liver quivering and my legs quaking. This was how I felt every time me and Shane had sex. He flipped me over onto my stomach before he drove his meat inside me again.

"Oh shit!" I cried as he drove into me harder and faster.

I was enjoying the feel of our sexual rendezvous, but I was a little nervous about telling him I was pregnant. The anticipation to tell Shane had me wanting to push him off of me. Finally, after what seemed like forever, he pulled out and laid beside me.

"Whew!" I blew out the air I had sucked in when trying to catch my breath.

Shane just laid next to me breathing deeply in and out. After several minutes of silence, I asked, "What took you so long?"

"I told you I wasn't sure if I'd come. If I didn't commit to coming through, how could I have taken so long?" He countered.

"I'm just saying. I had asked you to come through, so…"

"So, I still hadn't said I was coming. What the hell is so important anyway?"

I took a deep breath and tried to give myself a silent pep talk. *Just tell him He can either accept it or not, but you have to tell him. Maybe he'll be excited about the baby.*

I took another deep breath and he looked at me. "You gon' talk or what?"

"I'm pregnant!"

I had to get it out there before I changed my mind. I knew he needed to know because if I was going to terminate this pregnancy, I needed him to help me pay for it. He slowly sat up in bed and smoothed his goatee. "Say what, nah?"

"I'm pregnant," I repeated.

"For who?"

"What the hell you mean for who? Who the hell you think I'm pregnant for?"

"I'on know? Who else you been fuckin'?" He asked as he looked at me sideways.

"Oh woooow!" I said as I jumped up out of the bed. "Is this how we doing it?"

"I'm just saying. I know I ain't the only nigga bangin' that pussy out, so who the daddy is?"

My feelings were really hurt right now. Why was it that when a dude wanted to fuck, he always found a way to your bed, but when you told him you were pregnant, all of a sudden, the kid ain't his? I hated when niggas acted like that just because they were scared of responsibility.

"Actually, you were the only one I've been sleeping with for the past five months. I don't know what the hell you trying to prove or who you're trying to play, but this is your baby."

"I bet it ain't."

"Well, I know who I've been sleeping with it, so you can bet whatever you like. I can't believe you're acting this way," I said. I was devastated that he had reacted this way. But if he didn't believe my child was his that was all the more reason for him to help me terminate the pregnancy.

"Yea, well, you can get rid of it because I ain't about to take care of another damn kid!"

"I'd be happy to have an abortion because I don't need another kid either. I just need some help to pay for it," I said.

"Who supposed to help you pay for it?"

"I was hoping you would. This is your baby!"

"I ain't paying for no abortion!" He jumped out of bed and started putting his clothes back on.

"Really, Shane? You're just going to leave me to take care of this kid by myself?" I asked.

"What you mean? You just said you was getting an abortion!"

"I also said I needed help to pay for it. I called the clinic today and the lady said it would cost between 400 to 1500 dollars. I can't afford that shit!"

"Humph!"

"Humph what, nigga? If you don't help me get an abortion, you gonna have to help me take care of the baby because I ain't doing it alone!"

"Yea, well, you need to find the nigga who knocked you up to help you. I'm out!" With that, he chucked the deuces and headed toward the door.

I ran behind him because I needed his help. "Shane, please!"

"Please my black ass! I'm out!"

He opened the door and walked out. "You're a sorry ass muthafucka, Shane!"

"Maybe, but I ain't about to be a sorry ass muthafucka taking care another nigga's shawty!" He hopped in his Dodge Challenger and peeled out of the parking lot.

I went back in my apartment to check on my girls. Thankfully, they were still sound asleep. I went back in my bedroom and buried myself beneath the covers. I broke into tears because I was going to have to go through with this pregnancy. My feelings were so hurt because I didn't know how I was going to be able to take care of three children.

I cried myself back to sleep that night, hoping that tomorrow I'd get a miracle my way.

CHAPTER TWO

Cedrica

"We're having a baby!" I said as I jumped for joy in the bathroom.

I flushed the toilet and ran out of the bathroom with the pregnancy test still in my hand. I couldn't wait to see the expression on Marcus' face when he saw it. We had been trying to conceive for some time now, and after multiple wild sex sessions and late-night tricks it had finally happened. Marcus and I had been together for two years but had been close friends for almost five. Our relationship was a little complicated since he was a couple of years older than I was, but that still didn't stop nothing. If anything, the fact that he came with experience only made me want him even more.

"Quit lying Drica. Last time you said that, it was a false alarm."

"Well it ain't this time."

"Yea aight, then let me see the test," he replied.

I covered my mouth and shrieked with excitement as I walked inside of the master bedroom. I strolled over to Marcus, who was sitting on the edge of the bed rolling up and flashed the test in his face.

"Still think I'm lying?" I playfully asked as I placed the pregnancy test right on the tip of his nose.

"Come on man! Get that pissy shit out of my fucking face like that bruh! You know better than that shit!" He shouted as he slapped my hand and leaned back on the bed.

"Well you're the one who thinks I'm fucking lying. Hell, I thought you would've wanted an up close and personal view of the stick. It ain't like my pussy ain't been all up in your face before."

I sat on the bed next to him and grabbed the cigar out of his hand, then handed him the test. He sat up and grinned, then turned and looked at me.

"So, you finally managed to trap a nigga, huh?"

I stood up as I licked the cigar closed and glared at him.

"TRAPPED?! NIGGA, NOBODY TRAPPED YOUR ASS! IF ANYTHING, YOU TRAPPED ME!"

Marcus laughed and looked at the test again, then dropped it on the bed and stood up. He wrapped his arms around me and ran his fingers through my hair.

"Chill out. You know I'm just fuckin' around."

"Oh, I know," I sarcastically replied. "But don't ever try to play me like that. You know you wanted a baby just as much as I did, so if somebody got trapped, we trapped each other."

"Yea, yea, yea. Just don't make me fuck you up," he replied.

"What?" I asked as I dug in my back pocket for a lighter. "Fuck me up how and for what?"

"You know what I'm talking about. You know how you young hoes do when y'all get knocked up by a hood nigga with money. Y'all automatically see dollar signs and money bags, then start plotting on taking a nigga to court before the baby even born."

I lit the blunt and inhaled, then exhaled and laughed.

"Why would I take you court? You must plan to not take care of your child, cuz it's kind of early to be talking about all of this. What yo' ass really should be worried about is what your woman will say."

He snatched the blunt out of my hand and walked toward the bedroom door.

"I ain't gotta worry about shit, and neither do you. She already know what's up. But like I said, make sure YOU don't try to cross me cuz the problems that's gon' come after that ain't gon' be what you want."

I turned around and folded my arms.

"That's cool and all, but just make sure you don't try to cross me either. I'm not just your side bitch anymore. I'm the mother of your child, so I expect to be treated as such by you and her."

He inhaled and exhaled, then smiled showing off his pearly whites.

"I hear you. Just play your role and shit gon' be gravy for all of us," he replied as he walked out of the room and shut the door.

I rolled my eyes and spun around, then picked up the test. I wasn't too thrilled about being pregnant for Marcus, but I was happy as hell about the fact that I would finally be able to shit on the neighborhood hoes. They had been running their mouths about me and calling me names ever since they found out that I was fucking with him. Every time they'd see us together, they would make jokes about me being a sister wife or him robbing the cradle. It's like no one respected me or what he and I shared, but truth be told, they didn't need to.

I knew that our situation was fucked up from the jump, but I didn't care. Keisha was just the bitch he had been with since high school, so what they had wasn't really nothing. They were just comfortable with each other. But what we had was different. He understood me, and I understood him, and these hoes hated that.

The way he loved on me and broke bread with me made them sick to their stomachs. They didn't like the fact that Marcus treated me like a queen and treated them like peasants, but I had no control over that. Unlike them, I wasn't out there pushing myself up on every nigga that showed his grill or every nigga who whistled at me. I ignored them and made it a point to let them know that my body was a temple, not a trap house. Marcus loved that about me, which was why he chose me.

I walked over to the dresser and unplugged my phone from the charger, then unlocked it. When the screen lit up, I noticed that I had four missed calls from my homegirl Mai'lyn. I strolled over to the bedroom door and slowly closed it, then walked over to the sliding French balcony doors and stepped outside. Before I proceeded to call her, I looked around the property to make sure Marcus and his boys weren't outside. We were at a cabin in Helen, Georgia on a lil' couple's trip to celebrate their latest big move, but unfortunately, I didn't fuck with any of the bitches who were here. They were always gunning for me, so the last thing I needed was to have these hoes ear hustling and tryna sip my good tea.

Once I made sure that the coast was clear, I unlocked my phone again and clicked on Mai'lyn's name, then hit send. For her to have called me that many times, I knew something had to be up. I loved my girl to death, but Mai was like the neighborhood watch thot. She knew everything that was going on in and around the hood, simply cuz she was fucking everybody who rolled through that bitch. A lot of people didn't fuck with her, but she always kept me on my toes, so she was cool with me.

"Bitch!" she answered and yelled into the phone. "Why you ain't been answering my calls?!"

I sighed and held the phone close to my ear.

"Calm down girl. I was having an important conversation with Marcus."

"I don't give a fuck! I bet what y'all was talking about ain't more important than what I'm about to tell you!" She replied with worry in her voice.

I cupped my right hand around my mouth and looked around.

"What you talking about, Mai?"

"I'm talking about y'all need to leave from wherever the fuck y'all at right now!"

"What? Why?" I asked nervously as my heart began beating fast.

"Because Bitch! Keisha was just in the hair shop talking shit about you fucking her man and shit! Talking about her and her people pulling up on you and Marcus real soon!"

"What? Pulling up? That hoe knows better!" I shouted. "Besides, she don't even know we together. Marcus told her he had a lick out of town."

"Well, bitch, I don't know about all that. I'm just the messenger, but don't say I ain't warned you."

Next thing you know, I heard what sounded like a door getting kicked in followed by a loud scream.

"Hoe, didn't I tell you to stay out them people business?" A male voice shouted in the background.

"Boy, fuck you!" Mai replied. "I ain't in nobody business!"

"MAI!" I screamed into the phone.

Before she could even respond to me, I heard a bunch of shuffling and someone laughing then the call disconnected. I quickly ran into the bedroom and out of the door. As I hurriedly made my way through the hallway and down the stairs, my blood began to boil. Marcus assured me before we left that he had everything under control, but apparently, he didn't. When I got downstairs, I spotted him and his entourage smoking around a pool table while two bitches tongued each other down on top of it. I ran up to him and grabbed his arm forcing him and everyone else in the room to stop and stare at me.

"Drica, you aight, sis?" his boy Lucas asked me.

With my eyes still fixed on Marcus and my hands shaking, I rolled my eyes and shook my head no.

"Drica, what's up?" Marcus asked as he passed the blunt to Lucas and looked me in my eyes.

"I thought you told me you handled everything before we left," I replied as my voice cracked.

"What? I did. You buggin'!!"

"I'm buggin'? Is that why Keisha on her way up here right now?" I screamed.

"What?"

"Yea! You heard me! Mai just called and said..."

"Man look, fuck that h...."

"No!" I shouted. "There you go lying again nigga! I told you about telling the bitch about the moves we make! I didn't sign up for all that extra bullshit that she be causing!"

"What the fuck?" One of the bitches on the pool table said. "That powder must be something serious. Aren't you the side chick? Come here love. You need a hug baby."

"Yo Marcus, what the fuck she talking about son?" Lucas asked as he looked me up and down.

"ALL Y'ALL SHUT THE FUCK UP, AIGHT?!" Marcus yelled as he looked around the room.

He stepped closer to me and grabbed my chin.

"Is this some kind of joke?" He asked. "And don't lie to me."

"Does it look like I'm fucking lying?"

"Then how the hell that freak bitch knew where we was? Did you give her our location?"

"Are you fareal?" I screamed. "I didn't tell Mai shit! Keisha was in the nail shop talking shit about me as always and hollering about pulling up on us!"

He looked into my eyes and searched for deceit that he would never find. It didn't matter how close Mai and I were, at the end of the day I was still loyal to Marcus. She had asked me on more than one occasion where we were going, but I never told her. If I did, I would have been going against the code and against his dumb ass which was something that I would never do. But apparently, someone did. Marcus looked me in my eyes one last time, then let go of my chin and shook his head.

"Damn sis," Lucas grinned. "I thought you was better than that."

"What the fuck is that supposed to mean?" I replied as I looked at him in disbelief. "You can't really think I would do some shit like that."

He laughed and shrugged his shoulders.

"It ain't about what I think love. Yo' nigga know you better than I do, and from the looks of things you been running your dick suckers a lil too much baby girl."

"Nigga you got me fucked up if you think I would pull some shit like that! But if that's how y'all feel, then fine! I'll pack my shit and go! I didn't want to come here in the first fucking place!"

"Nah. You just tryna bounce cuz you know you guilty. See, this is exactly why I don't fuck with you young hoes. Y'all can never just be appreciative and enjoy the ride. Y'all always gotta be simple minded and try to get a nigga caught up."

I glared at Lucas and rolled my eyes. There was something about the look on his face that just didn't sit right with me. It's like he was happy and worried at the same time, not to mention the fact that he was being so cold to me. Out of all of Marcus's boys, he was the one that I was closest to, so the way he was coming at me was odd as fuck. I glanced at Marcus who was now standing against the pool table with his hands clasped together in front of him.

"So, I take it you believe him over me, right?"

"Drica..."

"No! For you to just stand there and not say shit proves to me that you don't really fucking love me like you say you do! Marcus, you know I would never in my life do no fuck shit like that! Ever! But since you want to believe your boy, you don't have to worry about me and my baby anymore! We'll be fine without this extra bullshit!"

I turned around and began making my way toward the stairs.

"Baby?" Lucas laughed. "You done knocked shawty up and she out here setting you up like that?"

Marcus sighed and looked at me, then turned to Lucas.

"She's telling the truth."

I stopped and turned around with a wet face, then looked at Marcus.

"What?" Lucas asked. "Nigga open your eyes and see the shit for what it is! Shawty set you up and trapped yo ass with a kid!"

"Nigga I did open my damn eyes! Drica telling the fucking truth!" Marcus yelled. "She ain't never lied to me about shit before!

So, my question to y'all is, which one of you motherfuckers let Keisha know where we was gon' be?"

"Nigga I ain't say shit," one of his other homeboy's named Jarin said. "But at the same time, you know Keisha always got a way of finding shit out."

"Nah! Fuck all that! Somebody snitched! So, who was it?" He shouted as he removed his gun from the holster.

"OH MY GOD!" The girls on the pool table shouted.

Jarin shook his head and walked up to Marcus.

"Bro think about what you doing. You don't even know if she really coming. Mai known for lying and making up shit."

Before Marcus could reply, there was a loud knock at the door.

KNOCK! KNOCK! KNOCK!

"Marcus, open this motherfucking door nigga!" Keisha shouted.

I threw my hands in the air and looked at him.

"What now?"

"Go upstairs and stay there!" He said as he tucked his gun back in his holster. I could see the serious look on his face and knew he was pissed. It was about to go down.

So much for that couple's trip…

CHAPTER THREE

Keisha

I was sitting in the beauty salon getting my hair done when my girl, Luna ran in with some fucking tea that made me split my fucking wig back. "Girl, you are not going to believe what I just found out!"

"Girl, what the hell could be so important for you to come up here during my hair appointment? You know how Shawndelle is about her clients chopping it up when she's doing my locks!"

"Umm hmm," Shawndelle said with an attitude.

"I'm sorry, but I thought you should know that yo man up there at the cabin with Cedrica's triflin' ass!" Luna said.

The words flew out of her mouth so fast, that I knew her tongue must've spiraled out of control and spat the wrong sentence. Marcus told me that he had a run to make with his crew. Nowhere in that informative conversation that we had did he mention anything about that bitch. He knew I couldn't stand that bitch because she had been a pain in my side since forever. I literally couldn't stand her and wanted to fight her every chance I got.

I was tired of beating her ass and tired of Marcus making me look like a damn fool. But I wasn't about to leave him. Not only was he sexy as hell at 6'4, 220 pounds of muscle with that smooth, chocolate skin and sexy ass, but the two of us had been together since forever and I loved him. I had a lot invested in that negro and no bitch was going to take what was mine. At the end of the day, I was the main bitch in his life and he was going to have to let the side bitch go.

"What the hell did you just say?" I asked as my blood began to boil. I just knew that Luna was lying to me. Sometimes, she had the tendency to get her facts screwed up. She was messy like that.

"You heard what I said. Your man is up at the cabin with his other bitch," she repeated.

"Shawndelle are you almost done, girl?"

"I'm halfway done!" She said with a huge chip on her shoulder.

She needed to get that shit fixed because I paid good money to get my hair done. Whether she finished the job or not, she was still gonna get paid, so she needed to get rid of that attitude. "Shit! It's cool though. That gives me just enough time to get my girls together, so we can head up there. I'ma fuck Marcus up if that bitch is over there with him, so I hope for his sake, he ain't there."

I pulled out my phone and hit up a few of my girls to meet me at the salon. As soon as Shawndelle finished my hair, we were gonna hop in my 2018 Cadillac Escalade that he bought for my birthday and head over to the cabin. I knew exactly which cabin Luna was talking about because I spent many weekends up there with him myself. For him to take that bitch to our cabin was a slap in the face, and that was exactly what he was gonna get when I saw his ass. Lord, I prayed that bitch wasn't there with my man because I was gonna catch a charge today.

Needless to say, Shawndelle took another two hours to finish my hair, and by that time I was close to flashing out. I paid Shawndelle $500 for doing my hair, along with a $60 tip and high tailed it out of there. Me and three of my friends, Luna, Alicia, and Fantasia hopped in my ride and I sped out of the parking lot on two fucking wheels.

"Damn girl! Slow the fuck down! I ain't trying to lose my life so you can catch yo man cheating once again!" Fantasia said with a laugh.

"Bitch fuck you! If it were your man, you'd do the same thing."

"If it were my man, I'd be in jail. Vince know I don't play that shit!" She said as she cracked up laughing.

"What the hell is so damn funny?" I asked as I looked at her in the rearview mirror.

"You are. I mean, how long has Marcus been fucking with that girl? And you still running up on him every time you find out they together. What's it going to take for you to put your foot down and make him stop cheating with her? I mean, damn, she must got a golden pussy or something!" The whole truck broke into laughter which made me wanna pull off to the side of the road and let them all out. I brought them with me for moral support, but I wasn't getting any of that right now. All they were doing was clowning my ass and I couldn't blame them. Shit, I'd do the same thing if the shoe were on the other foot.

"First of all, we don't even know that they're actually up there. Second of all, if you can't show me more support than that, I'ma have to let you out. This shit right here ain't cool," I said as I stared at her through piercing eyes.

"I'm sorry, Keisha, but seriously, what is it going to take for you to send Marcus' disrespectful ass packing?" Fantasia asked.

She had me fucked up. I had been with this man for eight fucking years. I couldn't just give up on him and throw everything that we had built away. I loved Marcus regardless of what we went through. We had been through too much for me to just give him up so that bitch could have him. I wasn't about to do that.

"I'm not about to keep defending my relationship with Marcus to you Fanny!"

"Well, explain it to me," Alicia said.

"Wait a minute... not you too. I mean, Shawn walks over your ass all the damn time, and you want me to explain my relationship. How about this? I'll explain mine to you when you can explain yours to me. Now, for the last time, I brought y'all with me for MORAL support. That means that y'all are here to lend an ear or a fucking shoulder to me. I don't need y'all questioning my relationship with my man... are we clear now?" I asked as I looked at all three of them. "Because if not, I can do this alone and y'all can walk back to the city."

"What?!" Fantasia shrieked. "Girl, you are definitely trippin' if you think I'm finna walk back to the damn city!"

"Keep it up and you will see that I'm dead serious," I said.

The rest of the trip to the cabin was quiet as fuck, just the way I needed it to be. I had a lot of thinking to do. I needed to figure out what I was gonna do once I got to the cabin and confirmed what Luna said. I didn't know how I'd react if I found out that bitch was over there. What I did know was that it wasn't going to be good for Marcus or her if that heifer was there.

♦ ♦ ♦

An hour later, I pulled into the driveway ready to beat the brakes off Marcus for lying to me. Even though I didn't know if Drica's stupid ass was inside, I knew that he lied to me about where he was going and why would he do that if he wasn't trying to hide something? I mean, he wasn't supposed to be at the cabin. Why would he not tell me he was going to be held up here for the weekend? I turned the truck off and took a deep breath.

"Are you sure you wanna go in there?" Alicia asked.

I looked over to my right and asked, "What the hell do you think?"

"I'm just saying… if ain't nothing gonna change between you and Marcus once you find Drica in there, what's the point of busting him?" She asked with a serious look on her face. She was right. If I was going to continue allowing him to treat me like this, why was I even here?

That question was easy to answer. I was here to fuck up what was left of his weekend and kick his ass, hers too if she was in there. "All I need to know is, do you bitches got my back or what?" I asked.

"You know we got your back. You don't even need to ask that shit!" Fantasia said.

"Fa real, we gotchu!" Alicia said.

"Hell, I'm the one who gave you the tea, so you know I got your back. Let's go in there and fuck shit up!" Luna said.

That was all I needed to hear. We stepped out of the truck and headed for the door.

BANG! BANG! BANG!

"Marcus open this motherfucking door right now nigga!!" I yelled.

I was so upset with him for putting me through this shit yet again. I waited for someone to open the door, but no one came after a couple of seconds. "I AIN'T GOING NOWHERE, SO YOU MAY AS WELL OPEN THIS DAMN DOOR!!"

A couple of minutes later, the door flew open and Marcus stood there looking like the cat that swallowed the canary. I barged my way in, followed by my girls and asked, "Where the hell is she?"

"What are you talking about Keisha? And what the hell are you and your little sidekicks doing here anyway?" Marcus asked.

I didn't have time for this shit. I began going through the cabin in search of that bitch. Marcus followed behind me as I went from the kitchen to the bathroom to the game room and finally the bedrooms. "What the hell are you looking for Keisha? You look like a damn fool right now!" He said as he continued to follow behind me as I went from room to room like a madwoman.

"You know exactly what I'm looking for!" I continued.

When I got to the last bedroom, he jumped in front of me. "Why don't you trust me?"

"Are you serious right now? You wanna know why I don't trust you when you're up at the cabin when you're supposed to be somewhere else! You have got to be kidding me!" I said.

"Well, maybe if you trusted me…"

"Don't give me that trust shit Marcus! I've trusted you and you've made a fool out of me more than once, including right now. I'm just gonna start going with my gut and instinct to tell me the truth. NOW MOVE!" I said as I pushed him out of the way. Before he could jump in front of me again, I turned the knob and opened the door. I didn't see the bitch when I first walked in, but I knew she was here because I could smell that knock off Chanel perfume she always wore.

That shit literally made my nose itch as I checked the closet and under the bed. "You are really doing too much!" Marcus said. "This shit here is why our relationship is so fucked up!"

"Nah, it ain't cuz of me that our relationship is fucked up. It's because of you!" I said as I moved toward the bathroom.

"Babe, you know I love you, right?" He said as he tried to block my path again.

"I don't wanna hear shit about that love unless I find this place clear of that bitch!" I said as I opened the bathroom door. Sure enough that bitch was in the bathroom, sitting on the toilet in hiding.

I looked at Marcus then back at Drica before I charged her ass. I knocked her ass clean off the toilet before she had a chance to get up. I guess everyone heard the commotion and came running because next thing I knew, I was being dragged off her ass. I was so pissed at Marcus, but mostly at myself for being such a fool. Drica finally stood up and looked at me as she rubbed her belly.

I looked from her to Marcus and asked, "What's she doing that for? Please don't tell me you were stupid enough to get that bitch pregnant."

As he stood with his mouth open, she stood there with a smirk on her face. "Since he doesn't seem like he's ready to tell you, allow me. WE'RE PREGNANT!" She shouted with a huge smile on her face.

My stomach and heart hit the floor with a thud. I couldn't believe that she was actually pregnant. Marcus continued to stand there with shit on his face as tears flooded my eyes. How could this be happening to me? How could he have gotten her pregnant when I couldn't even conceive? This shit was the worse feeling in the world. I wish I had never come here.

CHAPTER FOUR

Marcus

I didn't know what the hell Keisha was doing here. Hell, I didn't even know how she found out we were here. I told her that I was going out of town with my crew, so how did she end up here? Lord knew that I didn't need this drama in my life. I had enough with the fact that she knew I was fucking with Drica, but now Drica done opened her mouth about the baby. I hadn't even had time to process that shit before she went to running her mouth to my ol' lady. The look on Keisha's face hurt me to the core. I loved this woman with all my heart, but if I was to tell the truth, I loved Drica too.

I didn't know how I got caught up between two women, but I wasn't a dog like some people thought. I was just a man who crossed some boundaries with one of his good friends and didn't know how to go back to where we were.

"So, you got her pregnant?" Keisha asked with tears in her eyes. What the hell could I say? I surely wasn't trying to tell her the truth, not right here in front of every damn body. That wasn't no one else's business but our own.

Looking at Keisha all angry and shit had my dick getting hard. As I stared at the two women in my life, I marveled in some of their similarities. Keisha had her hair and nails done on the regular, and her makeup was always on point. She stood at 5'10, with those sexy long legs like a fucking gazelle. She was so beautiful with her beautiful brown eyes, high cheekbones, sexy lips, big breasts and perfectly round ass. I couldn't believe how fine she was even after three kids. She was bi-racial, her mom was black, and her dad was Hispanic, so you could imagine how beautiful our kids were. From the moment I saw her, I knew I had to have her with her naturally curly, black hair and that creamy hot chocolate skin.

"I think we should talk about this when we get home," I said, hoping that she'd go for that shit.

"Hell no! We're gonna talk about it right fuckin' now! Did you or did you not get this bitch pregnant?" Keisha asked.

"Watch who you calling a bitch!" Drica said.

As I watched Drica bite down on her bottom lip, my dick bounced in my pants. Drica was a couple of inches shorter than Keisha, but that didn't make her any less attractive. She had slim thighs, a plump round ass and nice round C cup breasts. Her peanut butter skin was what attracted me to her the most. She had a beautiful smile, but her eyes always looked like she was halfway asleep. She was still pretty though, to me anyway.

"Bitch shut the fuck up before I jump on your ass and knock that lil demon out of you!" Keisha said.

"You got me fucked up if you think you gonna come at me like that. Baby or no baby, we can do this!" Drica said.

"Ladies, y'all need to calm down!" I said.

"Marcus shut the hell up! This is all your fuckin' fault!" Keisha yelled. "How could you get this bitch pregnant?"

"You got one more time to call me a bitch..."

"BITCH! BITCH! BITCH! BITCH! BITCH! Now, what you gonna do BITCH?!" Keisha asked Drica. "Please feel froggish enough to jump, so I can mop the flo' witcho ugly ass!"

"UGLY?!" Drica shouted.

"D-d-d-d-d-did I stutter bitch?" Keisha asked.

"Keisha baby…"

"Don't Keisha baby me, motherfucker! I oughta knock your fuckin' teeth out your damn mouth!" Keisha fussed.

Her girls were standing around snickering and laughing. I really wished she hadn't brought those messy bitches with her. The whole city was gonna know what the fuck went down out here, especially with Luna's ass here. That bitch was just as messy as Drica's friend Mai. To be honest, I didn't know which was messier, but I do know that I regret coming here this weekend. I knew that Keisha wasn't going to let me off easy for this shit. Dammit!

"Keisha, calm down before you say some shit that get you fucked up!" I warned.

"Boy bye! You know what? I'm done!" She said as she raised her hands up in the air. She turned on her heels and walked out of the bathroom, then the bedroom.

"Wait! Keisha, what you mean you done?" I asked. She and I had argued about Drica plenty of times, but she never left me no matter how mad she was. She and I had this bond that no bitch could break.

"I mean, I'm done! I'm tired of you disrespecting me with that bitch! I'm just tired!" She said as she tore out the front door. I didn't wanna lose Keisha, but if I did, it would be all Drica's fault for telling her that she was pregnant. She should've kept her damn mouth shut and let me tell Keisha when I was ready. Why the fuck did she do that shit anyway?

"Keisha you know I love you…"

"LOVE?! YOU DON'T KNOW WHAT LOVE IS MARCUS!" She cried as tears streamed down her face.

"I do know, and I love you!" I said as I tried to reason with her.

"So, love makes you hurt me this way?" I hadn't even thought about it that way. I did love Keisha, but I didn't know why I did the things I did. I loved Keisha, but I cared about Drica. I mean, she and I had been through a lot also.

"No, but..."

"But I'm done!" She cried as she unlocked her truck. She hopped in behind the wheel as her bitches climbed in their respective seats. She started the truck and the engine purred to life.

"KEISHA, LEMME TALK TO YOU BABY!" I called out as I waited for her to roll the window down.

She didn't even bother to answer me as she put the truck in reverse. "KEISHA!" I called out as she put the truck in drive. "KEISHA!"

She didn't respond or look my way as she tore out of the driveway of the cabin. I ran my hands down my face as I watched the truck disappear around the bend. I turned toward the cabin and saw Drica standing on the porch smiling. I knew this shit would make her happy, but damn. At least try to hide your shit or keep it to yourself! I walked toward the porch, pissed that Cedrica had told Keisha the news about the baby. She should've waited and let me tell her.

"Why the hell you go head and do that?" I asked.

"She had a right to know," she simply stated.

"I should've been the one to tell her. You're fucking with my relationship big time, and I don't appreciate that shit at all!" I said.

"So, now it's my fault that your girl didn't take the news well?"

"You don't even get it fool! You shouldn't have said shit! That wasn't your place!"

"The hell it wasn't! This is my child!"

"Oh, so it's your child! Keep spitting that same shit when you have it, ya hear me?!"

"That's not what I meant..." she said as she tried to clean it up.

"That's what the fuck you said!"

"You're twisting my words," she said.

"I ain't twisting shit! I think you wanted to tell her so what happened would happen."

"Maybe. Now that she said she's done, we can be together," she said happily.

"Psshh!"

"What's that supposed to mean?"

"I love her Drica and you know that shit! No matter what the hell you and I have going on, at the end of the day, I love Keisha," I admitted.

"What about me? Don't you love me? I mean, you said you did," she said.

"Niggas lie all the time," Brandi said.

"Shut the hell up Brandi!" Drica said. "Nobody asked you for your fucking opinion!"

"You ain't gotta ask. I'm trying to help you out!" Brandi said.

"Brandi, mind your fucking business!" I said.

She turned and made her way back inside the cabin. I made my way inside and to the bedroom. I grabbed my suitcase and started shoving my clothes in it. "Where are you going?" Drica asked, her voice trembling as she spoke.

"I'm going home! I need to make sure that Keisha is good!" I said.

"You need to make sure that she's good?! What about me? I'm the one having a baby!"

"Yea, I know, but my concern right now is for Keisha," I said as I closed up the bag.

"So, you're just gonna leave me here?"

"Yea, my boys will make sure you get home safe. I'ma hit you up later!" I said as I grabbed my bag and walked out the bedroom.

"MARCUS!" She called from the bedroom. I just continued to walk while she continued to call my name. "MARCUS!! MARCUS!"

I didn't bother to answer as I went out the front door. I hopped in my all black Chevy Silverado and peeled out of the parking lot. Drica would learn that I wasn't the nigga to fuck with. She should've kept her trap shut. Now, she done ruined our damn weekend.

CHAPTER FIVE

London

After my run in with Shane, I didn't wanna do shit but climb in my bed and go to sleep, and that's exactly what I did until my phone started blowing up. I rolled over and picked up my phone from the nightstand, then shook my head and answered it.

"What is it?" I sighed.

"Hey girl! What you doing right now?" My cousin Drica asked.

She only called when she wanted or needed something, but now was not the time for her to need any favors from me. I wasn't feeling like doing shit after Shane left my ass high and dry. I was still having trouble understanding why he did that.

"I'm in my bed. What you want Drica?"

"Why you coming at me like that? Last time I checked, we were family!"

"Really? You gonna pull the family card, even though it's been weeks since I last heard from you?"

"I know, and I'm sorry about that. But I'm in a really bad situation and I need a ride…"

"A ride?"

"Yes, I need you to come get me cuz. Pleeease!"

"Come get you?!" I shouted as I sat up in bed. "From where?"

"Well, remember when I told you I had plans to go to the cabin with Marcus?"

"Drica, don't tell me you're still messing with that nigga? Ain't he still with that girl Keisha?!"

"Keisha ma ass! Yea, he still messing with her, but so what? Our relationship is too far gone right now, which is why I need you to come get me."

"I guess, but why can't he bring you back? Shit, he brought your ass up there!"

"London, please! I'll explain it to you when you come, but right now I really need to get the fuck away from here!"

I picked up my hand and balled up my fist. I really wanted to cuss her ass out for constantly letting the nigga play her over and over again, but I didn't want to leave her stranded. At the end of the day, she was still my blood and to be honest I too needed someone to vent to. I pulled the pink Momme Mulberry Silk cover from off of me and threw my legs over the side of the bed, then placed my hand on my forehead.

"Text me the address and I'll be on my way in a minute," I replied.

"I'm about to send it now! Thank you soooooo much!"

"Whatever. Just make this your last time, cuz I'm not gonna keep coming to your rescue every time you get yourself in some shit behind Marcus' ass."

I hung up the phone and stretched, then slid on my slippers and threw my hair in a ponytail.

"Fuckkkkkk!" I shouted.

I grabbed my keys off of my nightstand, then stormed out of the room and headed out. Luckily my mom had decided to keep the kids cuz had they been with me, Drica would've been assed out. When I got in the car, I opened up her text and plugged in the address. This bitch was almost two fucking hours away. What the fuck? Why the hell did I agree to go get her ass in the first damn place? Ugh!

"Oh, hell nah! Her ass better be ready to put gas in my car!"

I started my car and pulled off, then called Shane. I didn't really want to talk to him, but I wasn't about to be on the road for two hours with just my thoughts. Besides, I wanted to see if he had something to say after the way he dissed me earlier. But just as I thought, he didn't answer the phone. If he thought he was gonna get rid of me that easily, he had another thing coming.

"Uh, nigga, I don't know what the fuck kind of games you tryna play or what kind of bitch you take me for, but you really need to call me back! You got me fucked up if you think I'm just gonna sit back and go through this shit alone while you go on living your best life! Either you give me the money for an abortion, or your ass can fall in line and get on child support just like the rest of 'em! When you decide what you wanna do, hit me up! I'm not fucking playing with you Shane!"

I replayed the voicemail, then hung up the phone and leaned back in my seat. I didn't want any more kids, but I wasn't about to come out of pocket and pay for an abortion on my own. I didn't fuck myself and get myself pregnant, he did. So, he was gonna have to step up whether he wanted to or not. No sooner had I hung up the phone, was it ringing again. I wasn't surprised to see that it was Shane calling me back. I guess all it took was for me to read his ass for him to see that I was serious.

"I thought you'd be calling back," I sarcastically answered.

"This ain't Shane, but who's this?" A female voice who I didn't recognize asked.

"What?! How the hell you call my phone and ask me who's this?! Who the hell are you?"

"I called you back because you called my man's phone!"

What the fuck was this strange bitch talking about? How the hell did I call her man's phone when Shane was just in my damn bed less than 48 hours earlier? Since when was he her damn man?

"Your man? You must be confused…"

"I ain't confused shit! I heard the lil' voicemail you left him!"

"Okay? And?"

"You're crazy as fuck if you think he's about to give you anything."

"No bitch! You crazy for calling my phone with that fuck shit! I don't know what the fuck you think this is, but 'your man' gonna pay for this baby!" I yelled as I fought back the tears. How could this be happening a second time? Why was God punishing me this way? Didn't I deserve some happiness for a change?

The woman laughed.

"Lil' girl quit playing on his phone and go find your real baby daddy! You're not the first and I'm sure you won't be the last, but I'm here to tell you that you ain't about to see shit from Shane! Y'all hoes ain't tired playing these games?"

"What games bitch? I ain't playing no games this way!"

"You gotta be playing games if you think my man about to pay for anything to do with that lil bastard baby! You hoes always pull the same pregnancy card when he cancel y'all asses! It never fails!"

"First of all, I'm not a lil' girl and I'm for damn sure not a hoe! And second of all, nobody pulling shit or playing games! What the fuck?! I don't know who the fuck you are, but you sound stupid as hell taking up for a nigga that's constantly cheating on your ass!"

"Stupid?" she laughed again. "Shit, that's something I could never be. The shit that Shane does don't faze me, cuz unlike y'all I don't need that nigga. I get him when I decide I want him, and y'all hoes get him when I don't. But you wouldn't understand that sweetie, cuz if you did you wouldn't be in the situation you in now. What kind of bitch leaves a voicemail on a nigga phone begging for money for an abortion?"

"The kind of bitch that will fuck you up onsite hoe!"

"Yep. Trashy, just as I assumed. But I ain't got time to keep going back and forth with you love. I wish I could, but unfortunately, I gotta ride my man's dick before we get up for work in the next few hours. So, good luck with getting that abortion money and you have a nice night."

"BITCH, FUCK YOU HOE!" I screamed into the phone. "MAKE SURE YOU KEEP THAT SAME ENERGY LATER, CUZ IF I EVER RUN INTO YOUR ASS IT'S ON!"

She laughed and hung up the phone, leaving me sitting there fuming. I couldn't believe this nigga. Now I understood why he reacted the way he did when I told him about my pregnancy. He didn't want the shit to fuck up whatever he had going on with that bitch. It was too late for that though cuz I was gonna have my baby. I told him more than once about fucking over me. It was time to show him that there were consequences for his actions.

That bitch thought she was gonna have the last word, but we'd see who was laughing when she found out I was keeping my baby. Yea, I was gon' laugh my black ass all the way to the courthouse to file for child support as soon as I dropped that load. That bitch was gonna see that she fucked with the wrong one, and Shane... hell, his ass would learn the biggest lesson. I'd hit him in his pockets with so much force, he would wish he had called me back instead of his bitch.

♦ ♦ ♦

Two hours later, I pulled up to the location to find Drica already outside with her luggage. She quickly threw her things in the back seat and climbed in. "Thank you so much for coming to get me," she said. "I thought I was gonna have to kill one of those bitches!"

"What the hell happened? Why didn't you come back with the nigga who brought you here?" I asked, still frustrated that I had to get out of my comfortable bed to make a two hour drive.

"Girl, me and Marcus had a nice weekend planned, right? Tell me why his bitch showed up here!"

"Wait, I'm not understanding. What happened?"

"Keisha happened! Somehow, she found out that we were here and crashed our party!"

"Wow! So, what happened? Did y'all fight or something?" I asked because I was definitely curious.

"Nah, it didn't get to that point. I wasn't about to get in a fight with her and risk losing my baby," she said as she rubbed her flat stomach.

"Baby? Damn Drica, you let that nigga get you pregnant?" I asked.

How could she be so stupid? Shit, I was just as stupid as she was so how the hell could I call her stupid? We were both stupid as far as I could tell. Stupid for the D.

"I let him get me pregnant because we wanted a kid together! He wanted a baby by me just as much as I wanted one from him!"

"But he already has a woman. What kind of relationship are y'all gonna have now that you're bringing a baby in the mix?" I asked.

"We gon' have a good one. Sooner or later, he's gonna wanna be with me and his child and leave her ass. She can't give him what I can…"

"Girl please, any bitch with a pussy can give him what you can! You ain't special Drica!"

"Damn bitch! Who done pissed in yo Kool-aid with that stank ass attitude?"

"I'm sorry. Things haven't been going well for me either. I found out I was pregnant and told Shane about it. Let's just say he didn't take it well…"

"Hold up! You sitting here giving me grief about my pregnancy and relationship when you pregnant AGAIN?! How many that makes you… three?" Drica asked.

"First of all, it doesn't matter how many kids I have as long as I'm taking care of them. Don't nobody help me take care of my kids, so I don't have to justify how many I have to you or anybody else," I said. "And for you to come at me like that after I drove two hours to pick yo ass up…"

"Damn cuz! I wasn't trying to piss you off. I'm on your side," she said.

"Well, it sure doesn't seem like it. Anyway, Shane walked out on me when I asked him for money to abort the kid!"

"Damn! He just walked out and left you hanging?"

"Yea. On my way here, my phone rang, and his name popped up. I thought he was calling to tell me he had a change of heart and would give me some or all the money to have the abortion. It wasn't even him on the phone," I said as I blew an exasperated breath out.

Just thinking about that bitch calling my phone pissed me off all over again. The nerve of her ass.

"Who was on the phone then?"

"Some bitch who said that Shane was her man!"

"What the hell? So, a bitch called you from his phone?"

"Yep! Pissed me the fuck off, fa real!" I fumed.

"Shit, I'd be pissed too. When Keisha showed up at the cabin, I was beyond pissed. Then when Marcus left me there to go chase after her…"

"Hold up! Marcus left you at the spot where he took you to go chase after Keisha?"

"Yep…"

"Does he know that you're pregnant?" I asked.

"Yea and she does too."

"And he still left?"

"Do you see him here? Yea, he left anyway, but I ain't trippin' though. He'll find his way back to me," Drica said.

"We really are a pair, aren't we? We both pregnant by niggas who walked out on us. That's some bullshit!" I said. "Shane can run, but he can't hide. I'ma have this baby and take his ass to court for child support!"

I had plans to have an abortion if I could get the money together, but now that Shane had allowed some bitch to disrespect me, I was having this baby. Whether he liked it or not, he was going to be a daddy.

CHAPTER SIX

Drica

Did she just say that she was gonna drag Shane in court for child support? I thought she said she was trying to get abortion money from him. Maybe I misunderstood.

"So, you're keeping the baby?" I asked just to be sure I had heard what I heard.

"Hell yea! I'm not gonna have some bitch disrespecting me and thinking she can get away with it!"

"What do you mean? So, you're gonna let some bitch dictate you having a baby you aren't ready for? I mean, you're already raising two kids by yourself. Do you really wanna add another one to the equation?"

I was definitely confused as to how her bringing another child into her life would hurt anyone but her. She really needed to think that through because if she thought taking care of two was hard, taking care of three was going to be super hard. I couldn't imagine being in her shoes. This was my first baby and depending on how things worked out between me and Marcus would determine how many I'd have afterward. I wasn't about to strap myself with a brood of kids to prove a point to anyone because at the end of the day, a man could walk away from his child. A mother could never do that.

"At the end of the day, it's my decision to make."

"I understand that London, but you already have a hard time taking care of the two you have by yourself. What if Shane doesn't help you? What if he doesn't step up and claim your baby?"

"What if Marcus doesn't claim yours and help you? What are you prepared to do about that?" She countered with a smug look on her face.

"The difference between my situation and yours is that this is my first one. One baby as opposed to three kids should be a walk in the park. Look, I can see you're getting angry and I'm not trying to upset you. I'm just trying to get you to see how hard it's gonna be for you," I said.

"Thanks for your concern cuz, but I got this. Shane will be a part of my child's life whether he wants to or not," she said.

Yea, she was definitely delusional. Once she realized that what she expected to happen won't be happening, she'll get it. I mean, that nigga let a bitch use his phone to call and disrespect her. That meant he either lived with the bitch or their relationship was serious. I wondered why men treated women that way. Why would they allow another bitch to call the chick they been fucking in the first place?

Keisha had called my phone multiple times in the past. She had called to cuss me out so many times I had to add her to my block list. I was still pissed that Marcus had left me there to run after her. What made her so damn special anyway? I guess it was the fact that they had three kids and shit. But hell, I was having his kid too and he wanted a child with me. How could you want me to have a baby by you, but when it happens you duck and run? That didn't make any damn sense to me.

I decided to send Marcus a text because I knew he had made it home by now.

Me: Hey did you make it home yet?

I sat patiently waiting to see if he'd text me back. My phone began to ring, and I almost dropped it because I thought it was him calling me. But when I looked at my screen, I saw that it was just Mai calling. I knew she was calling for an update on the Keisha situation, so I wasn't gonna pick up.

"Ain't you gonna answer your phone?" London asked.

"Nah, it's just Mai."

"Yo, you still friends with that messy ass girl?"

"Yes, why not? She ain't never made no mess on me. Hell, if it wouldn't have been for her, I wouldn't have known that Keisha was on her way to the cabin before she got there," I said.

"I believe you. Leave it up to Messy Mai'Lyn to have all the business with her messy ass! I don't know why you still friends with her because sooner or later, she will stab you in the back too!"

I just rolled my eyes because I was tired of hearing about when Mai made mess about London. What happened between the two of them had nothing to do with me. That was their own business and I was happy to stay out of it. Besides, if London hadn't told her business to the lady at the nail shop, Mai wouldn't have had any business to tell. Sometimes, people needed to learn to keep their mouths shut. They acted like they had to tell their business to people in the nail and hair shop. Not me. I wasn't saying shit.

Marcus finally texted me back after I had been waiting anxiously for 20 damn minutes.

Marcus: Yea... u really fucked up yo! You told that Mai bitch where we were gonna be huh? U ain't gotta lie.

Me: Hold up! I already told you that I didn't say shit to anyone about where we were going.

Marcus: Then how did Keisha find out

Me: Idfk! Ain't you over there with her? Why don't you ask her?

"Damn! I guess that's Marcus you texting huh? You need to slow down before you set your keyboard on fire," London said as she giggled. I cut a sharp gaze her way letting her know if looks could kill she'd be a goner.

Marcus: I know that I didn't tell nobody that we were headed to the cabin so it had to be u, ma nigga

Me: I can't believe you're accusing me of some shit like that. I didn't do anything or tell anyone, but I guess that's how you're gonna do it to end things with me, right?

Marcus: Nobody saying all that. I'm just saying that yo ass is just as messy as that bitch you hang with. I know you told her ass where you were going and that shit is gon' cost you

Me: Cost me? What does that mean?

Marcus: You'll see

Me: No, tell me

He didn't text me back right away that time, so I sent another message.

Me: Marcus what does that mean?

I sat impatiently waiting as I thumped my feet on the floorboard of the car. I could feel myself beginning to sweat from the anticipation of his response.

Me: Marcus! Answer me!

I sent him about three more text messages, but he didn't respond to either. I guess he was mad, but I was mad too. How could he accuse me of telling Mai that? I never told Mai shit. I was tempted to, but I didn't because I knew if something like this happened, he'd blame me.

"What'd he say?"

"He said that I must've told Mai that we were going to the cabin and that she must've told Keisha. He's blaming me for his bitch finding out where we were," I said.

"Did you tell Mai where y'all were gonna be?"

"No! I didn't tell anybody!"

"Humph," she said.

"What does that mean?" I asked defensively.

"Nothing. But the fact that Marcus thinks Mai is responsible just goes to show that your friend ain't shit. That bitch is messy and she's gonna ruin your shit, if she ain't did that already," London said.

"Whatever. I didn't tell Mai anything. She was in the shop when Keisha said she was coming up to the cabin, so she called me."

"I guess. Something ain't right, I'm telling you. But you know your friend and what she's capable of, so that's on you," London said.

"Can we stop talking about this? I have a damn headache," I said. I sat in the seat trying to figure out if I made the mistake and told Mai where I was gonna be. I couldn't recall having mentioned it, so I just tossed that thought out of my head. I was innocent and so was Mai.

Me: So, when am I gonna see you again? Did Keisha move out?

I just had to message Marcus again because I needed to know what the deal was with him and Keisha. I needed to know if she had moved out or if her dumb ass was still there. If she knew better, she'd move out because I wasn't going anywhere, especially not now that I had Marcus' kid growing inside me.

Of course, there was no response. If he thought I was gonna let this shit go, he had another thought coming. We were having a baby and that wasn't going to change. He had better step up and take responsibility for our baby or else...

CHAPTER SEVEN

Marcus

Two weeks later...

Shit, I had been in the doghouse with Keisha since the day we came back from the cabin. It wasn't like it was the first time she put me there, but it was the first time she had given me the silent treatment for so long. If we weren't discussing the kids, we weren't discussing shit. She didn't care what time I got home at night either because she had thrown me out of our bedroom. She really wanted nothing to do with me. I had been trying to speak with her for days, but she wasn't having it.

Today, I was gonna try something different. I was gonna pick up some take out and flowers, get my mom to keep the kids for the night, and woo my woman back. Drica had been blowing up my phone like crazy and as much as I wanted to pick up and holla at her, I had to make sure shit was right with Keisha first. Keisha was the love of my life and we had three kids together. There was no way that I could walk out on them. We were a family.

Aaron was our oldest son at seven and he was the spitting image of me. Jalaya was our middle girl. She was six and looked exactly like her mom, but with my nose and eyes. And last, but not least, was Kennedy, my baby girl. She looked like me but had her mom's chino eyes and pouty lips. All our children were beautiful, well my daughters were. My son was handsome like me.

I had stopped by the jewelry store to pick up something I should've gotten for Keisha a long time ago. It was something that would seal the deal on our relationship and hopefully, alleviate some of her insecurities. As I made my way home, I smiled because I just knew tonight would be the night we made up. I pulled into the garage and hopped out of the car. I grabbed the bouquet of flowers, the jewelry store bag, and the food from Olive Garden and headed inside.

I showered and got ready for my woman to come home. She arrived at 5:00 and walked in to soft music, candle lights, and me holding the flowers in my hand. The look on her face wasn't even a happy or excited expression. She walked in wearing the same lame face she had been wearing for the past couple of weeks. She actually walked right by me and started calling for the kids.

"Jalaya! Kennedy! Aaron! Mommy's home!" she called out.

"Um, they aren't here," I said.

She turned to look at me, anger written all over her face. "Where are my kids?"

"They're our kids and they're with my mom for the night," I said.

"Since when? You didn't ask me if they could sleep out," she said.

"Ask you? They're my kids too Keisha. I don't have to ask you for permission to let our kids sleep over at my mom's. Are you crazy?" I asked. I could see her getting angry, so I tried to calm myself down because this wasn't how I wanted things to go. "Look, I just asked my mom to keep the kids for the night, so we could have some alone time."

"Really?"

"Yes really. I miss you babe," I said as I took a step toward her.

"You miss me? The reason you miss me is because you got that bitch pregnant! How could you do that to me Marcus? How could you do that shit to us?" She asked as her bottom lip began to quiver.

"I'm sorry babe. I didn't plan for her to get pregnant…"

"But you planned to stick your dick in her, right?" I stood there with my lips closed because nothing I said in response would make this better. She was right. "Exactly. What did you think was gonna happen if you raw dogged the bitch? You're old enough to know better. You are lucky I don't have any STDs because we'd be done for good!"

"I'm sorry, babe. I know I messed up…"

"Messed up?! No, messed up was when you started sleeping with that bitch!"

"We were on a break at the time."

"What about after we got back together Marcus? You still kept fucking her!"

"Keisha, no I wasn't."

She threw her hand on her hip and smirked.

"So, you gonna really stand right here in my face and lie to me? Like are you serious?"

"I'm not lying to you. I told you I only slept with her when you wasn't fucking with me. We was on a break."

"Break or not, you knew we always got back together."

"Yea, but…."

"But nothing! You shouldn't have fucked her! You can stand here and try to spin this shit around and use a break as an excuse, but the fact still remains the same! You slept with another bitch, and now she's pregnant!"

"I'm sorry Keisha, aight? I'm sorry! I don't know what else you want me to say or do to prove that shit to you! Yea, I fucked up! Yea, I shouldn't have fucked with her, but what's done is done! Ain't shit I can do to change what already happened!" I was rather frustrated by her attitude toward me. I thought we had put that shit behind us. Why was she bringing that shit up now? I guess because Drica had to open her damn mouth and tell her that she was pregnant. I wished Drica had kept her mouth closed.

"Yes, the fuck you can," she replied.

"No, I can't."

"Marcus, you can definitely change what happened, and you know how!"

"What you talkin' about? Like what the fuck you want me to do?"

Keisha cleared her throat and folded her arms across her chest.

"Make the bitch get an abortion!"

"What?"

"You heard me! Sit her dumb ass down and make her understand why she needs to have a fucking abortion! If putting a baby in her was something you didn't wanna do, then you shouldn't have a problem asking her to get rid of it!"

"Keisha I can't just fucking ask that girl to get an abortion. You know how I feel about shit like that."

"Oh really?" she asked as she raised her eyebrows. "That's funny!"

"And how the hell is that funny?"

"It's funny because you didn't feel shit when you asked me to get one!"

I dropped my head, then looked back up at her. She couldn't be serious right now.

"Come on man. Don't even go there."

"Nah! Fuck that! Let's address the shit like we should have done a long time ago!"

"We were in middle school, Keisha! We were fucking kids for God's sake!"

"So! What the fuck does that have to do with it? That would have been my first child, and you took that away from me! How do you think I felt?"

"Man, don't give me that shit. You were more than okay with it back when it happened. You know just like I do that we wasn't ready for no baby."

"Nigga, you don't know what the fuck I was ready for! And I didn't have a choice but to fucking be okay with it! You were so wrapped up in entertaining other hoes that you didn't have time to think things through or even talk about it! You brushed me off every time I tried to open up to you about what I wanted!"

"Whatever man. At the end of the day, neither you nor I were ready to be parents. It was either that or risk losing what we had in the process of trying to raise someone else when we barely knew how to take care of ourselves. Life was just starting for us, so that was really the only option."

"If that's how you wanna look at it, then fine. But now I'm telling you that this is YOUR only option," she said as she got all up in my face. "You can either tell the bitch to get rid of that demon seed, or you can choose not to tell her nothing and end up by your fucking self or with her triflin' ass!'"

"Hold up man," I laughed. "What you tryna say?"

"I ain't tryna say shit. I'm telling you exactly what it is. If she has that baby, you can forget about us and everything we've built. I will take the kids and leave."

"Quit fucking playing with me girl. You can't take my fucking kids away from me."

"Yea," she grinned. "I used to think that too but try me and see what happens. I'm done with this conversation."

She darted her eyes at me and walked away, then headed toward the stairs.

"Keisha!" I shouted. "Keisha, you can't give me no fucking ultimatum like that and just walk away!"

"I already did!" She shouted as she continued to walk away. "The choice is yours!"

"What kind of fucking shit is that? You buggin' my nigga!"

I stood there and watched as she ignored me and climbed the stairs. I could tell that she was hurt over the situation at hand, but she had me fucked up if she thought she was gonna just up and take my kids away from me. Whatever was going on between us didn't have shit to do with them. They were the innocent ones in this, but so was my baby with Drica. Getting her pregnant wasn't something I was trying to do, but that didn't mean I wanted her to kill our baby.

I mean, after all, shorty did stay down for me through all the shit I had been putting her through. Lord knew I put Drica through some shit with my relationship with Keisha. She stuck her neck out for me plenty of times, but then again, so did Keisha. I didn't know what I was gonna do, but I knew I needed to act fast. At the end of the day, it would be too hard for me to choose between the two of them.

CHAPTER EIGHT

Keisha

Finding out that the person that I had been loving through thick and thin was having a baby with another woman was devastating for me. Marcus and I had been through hell, but not once did I ever think he would do something as deceitful as this. Then to hear him say that he couldn't ask her to get an abortion was like a slap in the face. As a woman, I get the whole pro- life thing. But where was that energy when I had to go through it.

I was young, scared, and alone when I was forced to abort my first baby. Marcus wasn't even interested in becoming a father, nor was he willing to come and hold my hand while I went through that horrible, painful procedure. I still remembered that day like it just happened yesterday.

"What up? You ready?" Marcus asked as he sat on his silver and green Mongoose bike.

With a wave of tears in my eyes, I shrugged my shoulder and folded my arms. He sighed and put down his kickstand, then hopped off the bike and stood beside it.

"What's wrong with you?"

"Marcus, I'm scared," I replied. "I've never done this before, so I don't know what to expect. And on top of that, I'm just..."

"Keisha, come on girl. You can do this. It don't even hurt that bad. Erica get them done down at the same hotel all the time."

"I'm not Erica, and it's not the pain that I'm worried about. What if later on down the line, I start having regrets? What if I won't be able to have another baby when I got older? I have dreams of being a mom and having a nice house and stuff. What if once I do this, none of that ever happens?"

"Man, all we gotta do is have sex and make another one. It's easy," he laughed.

"It's easy for you cuz it's not your body," I said as I stood there with tears rolling down my face.

"So, what you wanna do, huh?" He asked irritatingly. "You really wanna have a baby in eighth fuckin' grade? You know how hard shit will be for us. We really won't be able to do shit no more. Is that what you want?"

"You don't understand."

"Nah," he said as he kicked his kickstand up and jumped back on his bike. "You don't understand. You never do. Shit, I'on know about you, but my dad will beat the black off my ass if he finds out I got you pregnant!" I watched as he shook his head in aggravation. "I took all my damn birthday and Christmas money to give you, so you can get that shit done! So you can do what you want, but if you don't go through with it, I want my fuckin' money back! I'm out!"

He shook his head and rode away, leaving me standing there broken hearted. What went down after he left was traumatizing to say the least, and it left me feeling empty. The next day, he came by to see if I had done it and told me not to tell anyone about what happened. I agreed to keep quiet thinking he would stay for a while to comfort me, but he didn't. He just kissed me on my forehead and left to go play basketball at the park with his friends. Just like a nigga... I was in here broken like a used toy and he was out there living his best life without a care in the world.

All I desperately wanted was for him to give me a hug and tell me that everything was going to be okay. But instead, he chose to run away and ignore the pain that I was forced to deal with.

Just like now. Instead of coming upstairs to check on me and console me, he decided to hop in his car and leave.

"I guess some things never change," I said as I looked out of the window and watched as he pulled off.

I already knew where he was going, but I was cool with it. Instead of getting myself all worked up, I chose to send him a little reminder message to make sure he understood that I meant what I said. I walked over to my Acme Furniture Vendome Gold Vanity Set and picked up my phone, then sat down. I went to my text messages and scrolled until I came across Marcus' name, then clicked on it and began typing.

Me: After everything we talked about, you chose to leave huh? I ain't even gotta ask where you going because I already know. But make sure you let that bitch know she what she gotta do. You already know what will happen if you don't, so be wise and make that your last time running to that bitch. I refuse to keep sitting around waiting for you to realize that your family needs you. THE GAMES ARE OVER!!!!

I pressed send and slammed my phone down, then looked in the mirror. I still couldn't believe that Marcus had the audacity to get Drica pregnant. Out of all of the bitches he could've fucked with, he chose to lay down with that slut. No matter how many times I catch him and beat her ass, he still continues to fuck with her. Things weren't gonna go down like that anymore though. I was tired.

I brushed my hair back behind my ear and looked down at my phone, only to see that Marcus still hadn't replied back. I guess he didn't have shit to say. It didn't matter though, cuz I had already made myself crystal clear. I got up and looked around the room, then sighed at the thought of how quiet it was. I hated the fact that my kids weren't here to cheer me up when I needed them most.

Twenty more minutes went by and there was still no word from Marcus. The pain that I felt in my chest from knowing that he was ignoring me while he was with that bitch was unbearable. The love of my life had betrayed me yet again…

CHAPTER NINE

Drica

I was sulking on the sofa when I heard footsteps coming down the hall. I jumped up because I hadn't heard anyone come through the door. I grabbed my baseball bat beside the entryway and waited to knock the brakes off whoever was in my damn house.

"Drica, where you at girl?" Marcus asked as he came around the corner.

I breathed a sigh of relief as I lowered the bat. What the hell was he doing here and why hadn't he called to let me know he was coming? After the way we left things the last time, I certainly didn't expect to see him now. I mean, he had stayed away from me for the past two damn weeks. He hadn't even bothered to call or text me to make sure that I was okay.

"What are you doing here Marcus?" I asked, pretending to be mad.

Of course, he had a key to my place. I had given him one about three months after we started messing around in hopes that things between us would grow serious, and that it had. A lot of good that did though. He still chose that bitch over me every single time.

"Don't be asking me no questions like that. I don't need a reason to come over here when I pay bills in this muthafucka!" He said sarcastically.

"Well, you don't pay all my bills, so I'ma ask again, what are you doing here? I haven't heard a word from you in two weeks and all of a sudden, you just show up at my place acting like nothing happened between us. Where have you been the past couple of weeks and why have you been ignoring me?"

"I ain't been ignoring you, but thanks to you opening your big mouth about your pregnancy, I've been dealing with a lot of shit!"

"Good!"

He smirked with his nose turned up in the air. "Good? What the fuck you mean good, Drica? I'ma need you to stop fucking with Keisha, ya heard me? She's my woman and we have a family together."

"What about us Marcus? What about me and the family that we're building together? This baby just isn't going to up and disappear ya know?" I needed to know what he was prepared to do for me and for our baby. His concern was always for that bitch. When was he ever going to be worried about me and my fucking feelings?

"Drica, I care about you, but you knew about Keisha before I even fucked. When we joked about you getting pregnant…"

"JOKED?! So, let me get this straight. When you and I were lying in each other's arms and we made the decision for me to get pregnant, it was a joke to you?" I asked.

"It wasn't a joke as in no 'ha ha, that's funny' type of shit. But I didn't think you'd seriously get pregnant!"

"That's a gotdamn lie! You weren't using condoms for a month…"

"BECAUSE YOU SAID YOU HAD THAT PATCH OR SOME SHIT! YOU SAID YOU WAS PROTECTED!" He shouted angrily. Damn. I knew I shouldn't have believed him when he said we'd be a family. He stood there looking at me for a good ten minutes. I guess he was waiting for me to say something to defend myself, but I couldn't. I just didn't know what to say and I didn't know if it would make a difference if I did say something.

"Say something, shit!"

"I'm just tired Marcus. I'm tired of being the side chick…"

"Aye, you knew what it was when we started fuckin'. Why you gotta act like that now?"

"Because I'm tired coming in second. I'm tired being ignored. If you really don't wanna be with me, then don't. I just don't think that I can do this shit anymore. My baby deserves more. He or she deserves better," I said as I rubbed my tummy. I was only 12 weeks along, but I was already starting to show. I loved looking at my body in the mirror, but now that I had a baby growing inside me, I was going to love it more.

My little baby bump was so cute, and I loved staring at it. Just knowing that there was a little somebody that Marcus and I created in there always made me feel warm and fuzzy inside. I was hoping that he and I would be able to share in this joyful experience together, but I could see that wasn't going to happen. He was so consumed with what was going on with Keisha that he had no room to worry about me. I loved him very much, but I wasn't going to put up with his shit while I was carrying his child.

"What are you saying Drica?"

"I'm saying that if I can't have all of you, I don't want none of you."

"What? Girl, quit playing. You pregnant with my seed, you think I'm just gonna walk away from my kid like that? Because if that's what you think, you'd better think again."

"Of course, I don't want you to walk away from our baby. You're a great dad. I want you in our baby's life…"

"That's what I thought…"

There it is. He thought he had won this fight, but I wasn't going to give him the satisfaction this time. "I just don't want you in mine."

The smug smirk he had on his face disappeared as he stared at me in disbelief of what I was saying. "What the hell you talking about Drica? Who the fuck you been talking to for you to come at me like that? Have you been watching that Iyanla show again? Because she can't fix shit with us because ain't shit to fix."

"I ain't been watching shit but you and Keisha make me look like a fool time and time again. I don't wanna be a fool anymore Marcus. You and I can co-parent our child together, but this shit, this fuckin' shit is done," I said. My insides were quivering like Jell-O because I didn't want things between us to be over. However, I knew if I didn't put shit out on the table this way, he would continue to take advantage of me. I just hoped that he didn't call my bluff and say okay.

"So, we're done?" He asked with a sly grin on his face.

"Yep, unless you want the three of us to be a real family, I'm done with your ass!" I said as I crossed my arms over my chest.

He took his shoes off as he bit slightly on his bottom lip. "You mean that?"

"Definitely. You can just leave my key on the table and go out the way you came in," I said.

He removed his pants as my bottom lip began to tremble. My heart began racing a mile a second as he continued to take off his clothes. Marcus knew that I was weak when it came to having sex with him. That was my biggest problem right there. I acted like he was the only nigga with a big dick. Shit, as much as I wanted to turn and walk away from him, I couldn't. I continued to stare at him as he stood there in nothing, but his boxer briefs and I could tell that his dick was hungry.

He moved towards me with a smile on his handsome face. He put his right hand behind my neck and pulled me in for a hot tongue kiss. That nigga's tongue was so deep in my mouth, he was touching past my tonsils. As he kissed me hard, he removed the skimpy shorts that I was wearing. It didn't take him long to press my back against the wall and insert himself inside me. I gasped as he lifted me off my feet and began to long stroke my throbbing pussy. Oh God! Why couldn't I just walk away after I said what I said?

He kissed me deep as his dick went in deeper. He pulled his lips from mine and asked, "You love me Drica?"

As much as I didn't want to answer him, my stupid mouth betrayed me. "Yes," came the voice barely above a whisper as he pulled my body off the wall. He was now holding me in the air and sliding my soaking wet kitty on his swollen shaft. He held onto my butt cheeks as he gave me the business.

"You still want me gone?" He asked as he pumped inside me with fervor.

"Um um," I mumbled because I was unable to verbally respond as my body shook from reaching my climax. He lightly sucked on my neck as he held me tightly. I was in absolute heaven right now and this was my problem.

Marcus guided us to the sofa and placed me on it as he climbed on top of me. He lifted my right leg on his left shoulder and pummeled inside me like a jackhammer to a sidewalk. When I was put in that position right there… lemme just say that I was never that weak until

Marcus started fucking me like that. As I cried out in pleasure, he gripped my hips and drove his dick inside me as far as it would go.

We were sweating like crazy as we made passionate love on my living room sofa for I don't know how long. All I knew was by the time he was done with me, I was purring like a cat. My pussy was throbbing, and my blood pressure was up. I curled up in a ball on the sofa as he sat next to me rubbing my thigh. We were breathing heavily as we relaxed on the sofa.

"Whew!" He said as he smacked my bare ass.

"Ow Marcus!" I cried out.

"Shit, you wasn't saying 'ow' a couple of minutes ago."

"Well, that's cuz you was all up in me and shit," I said.

"Damn girl, that pregnant pussy gon be the death of me over the next few months."

"Whatever," I said with a smile.

"I'm fa real. Go get daddy a beer, would ya?"

I slid off the sofa and walked to the kitchen, making sure to twist my ass extra hard because I knew he was watching me. I grabbed the beer from the fridge and turned around to find Marcus standing in the doorway stroking his swollen dick. "Uh uh, I need a minute to catch my breath," I said.

He smiled as he walked over to me and lifted me up on the kitchen counter, inserting his shaft inside me once more. I dropped the bottle of beer on the floor and it smashed loudly. That didn't seem to bother Marcus though as he slammed inside me over and over again. I didn't know what the hell he was trying to do, but whatever it was, he was definitely winning. By the time we were done, I was exhausted and ready for bed. He carried me to the bedroom and went to the bathroom. I must've drifted off to sleep because when I woke up, the sun was out, and Marcus was gone.

"Dammit!" I cried as I slapped my hands against the comforter.

CHAPTER TEN

London

It had been a whole month since I last saw Shane, but I had news for him. I wasn't about to be ignored through this entire pregnancy. I knew that he was gonna be at the barber shop today because he went to cut his hair the same time every other week. He had a standing appointment with his barber and that was fine with me. As I dressed myself all cute and shit, I thought about his reaction when we'd come face to face. I knew he'd be upset about me putting our business on front street like that, but I didn't care. He hadn't been doing right by me and I had enough.

I slid in my car behind the steering wheel and made my way to the shop. If I played my cards right, he'd be in the chair and wouldn't have a choice but to listen to me. 20 minutes later, I pulled into the parking lot and parked. I spotted his grey Ford F-150 and smiled because at least he was here. I checked my hair and makeup once more in the visor mirror before I got out of the car. I was just so tired of men walking over women like we weren't shit. Today, I was going to take a step in the right direction for all women, Drica included, because she had been letting Marcus use her as a doormat for the longest.

I walked in the barber shop and all eyes were on me as the dudes up in there tried to figure out whose ol' lady had made her way up in their spot. "May I help you?" One of the barbers asked.

I spotted Shane in the chair, but he hadn't spotted me yet. "Uh uh, I already found who I came for!" I said as I walked over to where Shane was sitting. "SHANE!" I called out.

He looked at me in the mirror and rolled his eyes. "Aw shit!" He mumbled.

"So, you can't return none of my calls or texts, huh?"

"You wanna go handle ya business, bro?" asked Tommy, his barber and friend.

"Nah, she need to get the fuck outta here!!" Shane said as he glared at me in the mirror.

"I ain't going no fuckin' where until you take responsibility for this baby!" I said.

There were a lot of 'aw shits' in that barber shop when I said that, but I didn't give a fuck. I wasn't beyond putting my business on front street for the world to know. That nigga had been playing me to the left since his bitch called me, but what they both failed to realize was this kid was mine and Shane's. It had nothing to do with that bitch who called me from his phone.

Once I said the word baby though, all of a sudden, he jumped out the chair. "I'ma be right back man," he said to Tommy as he grabbed me by the upper arm and dragged me out the shop.

"LET GO OF ME SHANE!" I yelled as I tried to break his grasp.

He flung the door open and pulled me behind him, dragging me all the way to the side of the building. He glared at me as he seethed with rage. "Why are you here?" He asked through clenched teeth.

"You already know why I'm here! You need to take responsibility for our child," I said.

"Ain't no child! You said you was getting an abortion!"

"No, what I said was you needed to help me pay for an abortion."

"And I didn't since I ain't that baby's daddy. Look, keep that kid if you want to, but you on your own with that shit!" I couldn't believe he was saying that to me. What had I done to deserve another deadbeat daddy for my kid?

"You already know who my baby daddy is. Even though you trying to make me out to be a hoe I ain't one! I knew who I was sleeping with and you the only one," I said.

"Get the hell out of my face with that shit London! I got shit to do!" He said as he waved me off.

"I'm not just gonna disappear Shane, and you will take care of this baby!"

"The fuck I will! You gon' take care of YO baby!"

"THIS IS OUR BABY! I DIDN'T LAY BY MYSELF AND MAKE THIS KID!" I yelled in frustration.

"I didn't make it with you, so you better get the fuck on and go find yo real baby daddy!"

When he turned his back to me and started walking away, I lost it. I ran up on him and punched him hard behind the head. "You won't ignore me or disrespect me Shane! This baby isn't going away and if you won't take care of it voluntarily, I'ma take yo ass to child support court and we can get the white people involved. I ain't scared to get those white folks in our business!"

He ran up on me so fast, I thought he was going to choke me, but all he did was get up in my face. "Lemme make myself clear to you. If you expect me to pay anything for that kid, you gon' have to take my ass to court. I'll be damn if I just come off my hard-earned money to some other nigga's kid. I ain't one of those niggas you can just back into a corner. I ain't gon' cave, so you can kiss the root of my black ass!!" He said as he glared at me.

"Why is it so hard for you to own up to your responsibilities?" I asked as my tears rose to the surface.

"I ain't owning up to shit! Do whatever you feel the need to do, but right now, I need you to get the fuck up outta here. I ain't got time for this shit no fuckin' more!"

He turned to walk back inside and that time I let him. What else was I supposed to do or say? He had already told me several times he wasn't gonna claim my baby. He could run if he wanted to, but there was no way he was gonna just ignore us. That shit would last as long as I was pregnant. Once I gave birth, fuck that! He wouldn't have a choice but to admit it was his baby.

And whoever his bitch was that called my phone, she was definitely in for a surprise if she thought I was just going away. Shane and I were connected for life, and I wasn't going any fucking where. I'd be lying if I said his words didn't hurt though. Every time he said go look for your real baby daddy, that shit stung. Every time he said he wasn't the daddy, I cringed. My feelings were just hurt, and my heart was broken.

As I sat in my car, I allowed my tears to surface. As they began to spill from my eyes and on my lap, I replayed the words that Shane had said. I hated the fact that I'd have to take care of my new baby by myself until Shane was proven to be the father. That meant, I was going to have to go through this pregnancy alone too.

Ugh! Why did it have to be this way? Why couldn't Shane just step up? Why did he have to be forced like the other two? Why wasn't I worthy enough to find a good man?

I thought what Shane and I had was real. I thought I was special. Now, I knew that I never meant shit to him. Why was I such an easy target when it came to men? Why did I let them use me the way that they did? What was it going to take for me to start putting myself first? Now, I was going to be stuck raising another baby by myself. That shit sucked so bad, but I knew what I was capable of.

I hadn't told my mom that I was pregnant yet because I knew she'd have a fit and a cow. She had been helping me ever since I gave birth to my first daughter. I didn't even know how I was going to break the news to her again. She had told me to tie my tubes when I had my last little girl, but I couldn't do it. It just seemed so final and I thought what if I got married one day and my husband wanted to have a baby with me. Would he leave me if I couldn't give him one?

How would I explain to my man that I couldn't give him a baby because I had two already? Now, I was going to be strapped down with a third baby and no daddy to help me. This shit sucked. Hell, it sucked being a woman because we couldn't just walk away from our responsibilities like men could. If we walked away the way they did, we'd be on trial for abandonment. I'd never walk away from my kids anyway. They were the most important little people in my life and I loved them so much.

As I sat here crying, my heart hurt so much to the point that I wondered if I'd ever be able to stop crying. Sometimes, life sucked big time. This was one of those times.

CHAPTER ELEVEN

Shane

I had no idea that London was gonna pop up and do some stupid shit like that. She knew what it was when it came down to our lil' situationship, so I wasn't about to let her pin no fucking baby on me. I walked back in the barbershop and all eyes were on me.

"Yo' Shane, you good cuz?" Tommy asked grinning.

"Yea, I'm cool. Just had to handle some shit real quick," I said as I sat back down in the chair. "Everything straight."

"Ya sure? Cuz shorty seemed hella pissed."

"I'm positive. She gon' be aight. It wasn't nothing but some miscommunication."

"Miscommunication my ass nigga! She handled you!" One of the other barbers shouted before bursting out in laughter.

"I'm saying though! I was scared for that nigga like that was my bitch or something," Another guy said while laughing.

I shook my head and clenched my jaw.

"Say, you just gon' let them niggas rip you like that?" Tommy asked as he stood there grinning.

"Man, I ain't worried about that shit. I got enough to deal with."

"Like what? What's up? Cuz that shit that just happened ain't cool man."

"Don't you think I know that?"

"Aye, don't get all tight with me homie. I'm just saying. It's not every day that a bitch run through here talking about a baby. On the other hand, you know people be talking. You wouldn't want that shit to get back to Renee."

I took a deep breath and swallowed hard.

"That ain't my baby."

"Oh now you talkin'," Tommy laughed. "Aight."

"Nah, serious shit. It ain't my kid. She got about four different baby daddies already. The bitch just mad. That's all."

"Mad for what though? I thought you and Renee decided to settle down," he said as he turned the clippers back on.

"We did, but this bitch wouldn't leave me alone. So, I ended up falling back into my old ways and fucking with her every once in a while. Now she running around telling motherfuckers she pregnant for me and shit. Calling my fucking phone all hours of the day and night, and leaving voicemails. Shit crazy man."

"Bro you know how these hoes do. You give 'em an inch then they end up wanting the whole damn dick. Once you let 'em go they play that role."

"I know that, but my girl don't. She got ahold of my phone one night and heard one of the voicemails she left. It's been trouble ever since. I keep tryna tell her that the bitch is lying, but she ain't hearing me."

"I feel you man. Look, at the end of the day, all you gotta do is stick to yo' word and stay away from the broad. Yo' girl gon' trip regardless cuz you was fucking around on her. But once shorty have the baby, get a test done on that lil' motherfucker. Then go from there."

"Yea, you right. I just wish I would've listened to my first mind and left that hoe where she was. Ever since I started fucking with the bitch shit been bad."

"That's usually how it is," Tommy laughed. "Nothing good usually comes from fucking with a hoodrat. Where you met her at anyway?"

"Nigga to be honest, I don't even remember. But if I could go back, I'd bypass that hoe like cancer."

Tommy laughed and finished up my head, as I sat there in deep thought. I knew exactly where I had met London's dumb ass, but I wasn't about to speak on that shit. I didn't need any of these niggas tryna build a case on me to present to my girl. She was already in her feelings with the whole baby situation, so finding out that I had met London at her birthday party would really fuck shit up. I wouldn't be able to explain that shit.

I mean, London wasn't invited or nothing. She was just there as a plus one, but still. Renee would look at that as the ultimate disrespect and leave my ass high and dry. I couldn't afford to let that happen. Not after all the money I had invested in her ass.

When Tommy was done, I paid him and dapped him up, then flew out of the shop. I ain't gon' lie, I was embarrassed as hell. But I was really anxious to get to London's fucking ass. That stunt she pulled at the barbershop was fucked up, and I was gonna make sure I let her know that before I did anything else. I leaned next to my car and pulled out my phone, then went to my call log and clicked on her name.

"What?" She answered with an attitude. "Didn't you say enough?"

"My nigga don't what me! What the fuck you did that shit for? Huh?"

"Because! Like I said, you've been ignoring me and disrespecting me and acting like I don't exist, but you got the right one! You ain't gon' be able to get rid of me that easily!"

"Ain't nobody been ignoring you girl! I've been busy!"

"Yea, I'm sure you have, seeing as how you have another bitch and all! You lied to me Shane! You told me that you was single when I met you! Now all of a sudden, you got bitches calling me back and shit! You got me fucked up nigga!"

"What?!" I shouted. "Nah! You got ME fucked up! Your baby ain't mine London! So miss me with that fuck shit! You fuck with all kinda niggas, but you tryna put that shit on me! It ain't happening! So you can stop showing up to where I be at! Stop blowing up my phone! And stop telling people that bullshit about me being your kid's daddy!"

"Nigga you can kiss my fucking ass, and kick rocks with them tired ass Nike slippers you got on! I'ma do what I want no matter what you say! And as long as this baby is part of me, it will be part of you! So stop playing with me Shane!"

"Bitch, you and that baby can suck my dick! I said what I said! Keep it up London and watch what happens to you! You playing a dangerous game my nigga! Quit while you ahead!"

"WHAT?! ARE YOU THREATENING ME?!" She screamed into the phone. "ARE YOU THREATENING TO HARM A PREGNANT WOMAN?! CUZ BITCH I WILL CALL THE COPS ON YO ASS REAL QUICK!"

"Good! Call 'em and tell 'em to help you find your baby daddy, and quit fucking playing with me!"

I hung up the phone and threw it in the car, then placed both of my hands behind my head. This bitch was really starting to drive me crazy. It was like there was no talking to her ass. Even when I tried to be cordial, she could never just shut the fuck up and listen.

"WHAT THE FUCK DID I DO TO DESERVE THIS?!" I yelled out.

Suddenly, a red Honda Accord pulled up beside me. I looked over my shoulder and instantly started fuming. I rolled my eyes as London hopped out of her car.

"What the hell you was talking on the phone?" She asked as she ran up on me.

"What the fuck you doing here girl? I'm done talking to you!"

"Well, you ain't gotta talk, just listen…"

"I AIN'T LISTENING TO SHIT!! NOW TAKE YO OL' RAGGEDY ASS HOME WITH THAT BULLSHIT!!" I said as I prepared to get in my car.

"YOU'RE GOING TO TAKE RESPONSIBILITY FOR THIS CHILD EVEN IF I HAVE TO GET THE COURTS INVOLVED!!"

"WHAT?! You better go talk that court shit to some other nigga!"

"I'm talking to my baby's daddy! WHO THE FUCK SHOULD I TALK TO?!" She screamed as she jumped up and down like a fucking bullfrog. "Oh, I know who I'ma talk to. How about I have a conversation witcho bitch?"

"Girl, GET OUT MY FUCKIN' FACE YO!!" I was trying my best to keep myself cool, but she was making me go somewhere no man should ever go with a bitch. I literally wanted to smack her upside her fucking head. I took a deep breath and opened the door to my car. I slid in and shut the door.

BANG! BANG! BANG!

"OPEN THE DOOR BITCH! GET OUT THE CAR WITCHO SORRY ASS!!" She hollered as she banged on my driver's side glass.

I just started the car up and backed out the parking spot. She continued to cuss at me and scream at the top of her lungs, but I kept going. That bitch was fucking crazy, but I was crazier than her. If she wanted to play it like that, she'd soon find out that two could play that game.

CHAPTER TWELVE

Marcus

With all the shit that I was in between Keisha and Drica, I had been having a hard time keeping my head on straight. Things were good on the home front, but I knew it would only be temporary. Instead of telling Drica to get the abortion, I decided to just roll the dice and not say nothing at all. I knew that it was fucked up and Keisha would eventually find out, but I was gonna cross that bridge when I got there. Until then, I made sure to keep the two of them away from each other as much as possible.

I pulled up to the gated community and pressed the buttons on the intercom, then waited for someone to answer.

"Yea," a man picked up.

"Yo' Pops let me in," I replied.

Without responding, he began dialing. When the gate opened, I pulled in and drove around to my parents' house. It had been a minute since I had been over there, so we had a lot of catching up to do. I pulled into the driveway and shut the car off, then hopped out. As I walked up to the door, my pops opened it and stepped out with a huge grin on his face.

"Long time no see, huh? I thought you had forgot about us."

"Not at all. Just been going through a lot."

"I'm sure you have. That's the only time you come around."

"Yea," I replied dryly.

I wasn't in the mood to deal with his sarcasm, but saying anything else would've only made things worse.

"Ma here?" I asked as I stood there with my hands in my pockets.

My pops folded his arms and leaned back a little.

"Nah. She took your kids out for ice cream and to the park to keep them busy."

"Oh, I was wondering why it was so quiet in here."

"Yea, you know those kids have no home training when they bring their lil asses over here," he said as we laughed. "Why? Something on your mind? Cuz you can always talk to me. You always wanna run to your mama like you ain't got two parents. I'm your parent too son, which means you can talk to me also."

"It ain't like that."

"I hope it ain't. Cuz you know you can come to me about anything. But I tell you what… I'm not gon' be all soft and easy on you like your mama though. You a grown man now."

"I know Pops," I said while nodding.

"Just making sure. Now come inside so we can talk about whatever you got going on."

He turned around and walked back in the house with me on his heels. When I got inside, I stood by the door and looked around. He closed the door and motioned for me to follow him to the basement.

"Come on man. Quit acting like you a stranger or something. You making me nervous shit."

I shook my head and walked down the stairs to the basement. That nigga ain't never changed, which is why I ain't really wanna have that conversation with him. Don't get me wrong, he was cool as a fan and always had my back. But he was also throwed. At times he reminded me of James from *Good Times*.

I sat on the black leather couch and leaned forward with my hands hanging in my lap, as he grabbed a couple beers out the mini fridge. He walked over to me and handed one to me, then plopped down on the couch beside me.

"So what's up young blood?" He asked as he cracked open his beer. "What's been going on in yo' neck of the woods?"

"A lot Pops," I replied. "Too much for one nigga to deal with."

"Uhm," he said as he took a swig of his beer. "That's how it is when you tryna juggle two women and don't know what you doing."

"What?" I smirked. "I ain't been juggling two women. I'm still with Keisha."

"So you gon' sit yo' black ass beside me and lie? Or you gon' be a man and be real about yo' shit? Cuz ya mama already told me what's going on with you."

I placed the beer on the table beside me and raised my left eyebrow.

"What you mean? What she tell you?"

"It ain't about what she told me. It's about what you gon' tell me," he replied. "We can keep going in circles until the cows come home, but I ain't saying shit until you tell me what's up son."

He took another swig of his beer and looked at me out the corner of his eyes. I put my head down, then looked back up. I didn't wanna have this conversation with my pops because he wouldn't agree with some of the choices I had made. But at this point, what choice did I have?

"I'm in a situation Pops. I cheated on Keisha with Cedrica."

"Again?" he asked. "That ain't nothing new."

"She pregnant this time."

"Who's pregnant... Keisha?"

"Nah. Drica."

"Oh. Cuz I was about to say. That crazy motherfucker don't need no more kids. Y'all got enough with the ones y'all already got."

"I don't know what to do Pops."

"You need to tell the fucking truth. That's all to it. Keep lying and you gon' stay in the shit."

"It ain't that easy though."

"It's easy enough to lay down with her, so it should be easy to stand up and be real. You can't keep running every time you fuck up. That's not what men do, and I didn't raise you to be less than one. You made your bed and now you gotta lie in it."

"But I don't wanna hurt nobody. That's the hard part."

"This might sound fucked up, but my boy, you gon' have to hurt somebody. Whether it's Keisha or Drica, I don't know. But you gotta make a choice. Cuz if you don't, you gon' end up alone and paying child support out the ass. You keep planting them seeds, every dime you gon' make gon' go to yo kids. So, you gotta figure out what or who matters most and let the other one go... for good."

I nodded my head and sat back on the couch. I hated to admit it, but he was right. At some point, I was gonna have to make a decision. The worse part about it though was having to choose with kids involved. I grew up in a tight knit family, so turning my back on any of my kids was out of the question. I looked at my pops and exhaled.

"Keisha told me to tell Drica to get an abortion."

At the sound of those words, he instantly began choking on his beer.

"WHAT THE FUCK?!" he shouted. "THAT MOTHERFUCKER DONE LOST HER DAMN MIND! AIN'T NO GRANDCHILD OF MINE GETTING ABORTED! I DON'T GIVE A FUCK WHO CARRYING IT! I HOPE YOU PUT HER ASS IN HER FUCKING PLACE, CUZ THAT'S SOME SICK SHIT!"

"I didn't tell her nothing. I just left the crib and went to Drica."

He slammed his beer down on the table and jumped up.

"TO DO WHAT?! I HOPE NOT TO TALK HER INTO DOING THAT SHIT!"

"Nah Pops. Chill. I ain't even mention it."

"So whatchu go over there and talk about? Never mind. If y'all talked much, she wouldn't be pregnant right nah. Look son, you're an adult now. You have to start making better decisions with this head." He tapped on my forehead with his forefinger. "And stop thinking with that head." He pointed to my main man, the one that had been making the majority of my decisions for the longest time.

"I know Pops, but it ain't as easy as you make it out to be."

"Aye, it wasn't easy for me either at one time, but you don't see me with 10 baby mamas…"

"Pops I don't have 10 baby mamas!"

"Right, I know I'm exaggerating a little, but you get what I'm saying. You have to make a decision and choose either Keisha or Drica, but you can't have both. I'm not sure who you're trying to build a life with, but whichever one you choose, make sure it's the best decision for you and your kids," he said.

"Pops I wanted to ask Keisha to marry me…"

"So, you wanna marry Satana?"

My pops always called Keisha the daughter of Satan because he said she had evil and spiteful ways. He was right. Sometimes, she did have ugly ways, but I drove her to behave that way. I was the one who made her come out of character. Keisha was a good girl and we made a good team.

"I love Keisha, Pops. Her name is Keisha. She's gonna be your daughter-in-law, so you need to respect that and her."

"I respect her. You need to respect her since she's your woman. If you want to marry her, you need to learn to respect her and stop cheating on her," he said.

"I know Pops."

"So, you said you were going to ask her to marry you. What happened? Did you change your mind?"

"Nah, before I could ask her, we started arguing about Drica and she ordered me to tell Drica to get an abortion."

"That's a sign son. That's a sign that you don't need to marry that woman. Any woman who would tell you to have your seed killed ain't no good woman!" My pops was pissed because he banged his hand on the table and everything. I understood where Keisha was coming from though. We had a life together and a family already. We had been together since middle school, so I was sure she felt threatened by another woman carrying my child.

"She is a good woman Pops. It's because of me that she's been put in that unfortunate situation! I mean, think about it… if you were cheating on mom and you got the other woman pregnant, how would mom feel? How would she react to the news of another woman carrying your seed?"

"First of all, your mom would murder my black ass!" He said which caused both of us to break into laughter. As genuine and wonderful as my mom was, he was right. She would have a cow if he cheated on her and got someone else pregnant. My mom did not play that shit.

"You're right about that!" I said.

"Shit, I know I'm right. Yo mama don't play that cheating mess. I remember this one time I stepped out on her..."

"Wait a minute... you cheated on mom?"

"Aye, I was younger, and I wasn't sure of my feelings for her. You know, kinda like you with the two females you messing with. You must not be sure of your feelings either, so you keep jumping from one to the other."

"No Pops, I'm sure of my feelings for Keisha. I really love her!" I said.

"Well, if that's true, how come you keep screwing that other girl?"

"I don't have an answer for that. When me and Keisha get along, we really get along great. But when it's bad, it's really bad..."

"So, you run to the other chick when shit bad with your woman?"

"Kinda."

"You gotta stop doing that son. You gotta man up and learn to talk shit through and work it out. If Keisha is the one you wanna be with and marry, stop cheating on her. Sit down and talk shit out with her and then, talk to that Drica girl. Let her know you gon' be there for your kid, but that's it. No more dick for her," Pops said.

I thought about what he said and realized that he was right. I was 28 years old and not getting any younger. I wanted to ask Keisha to marry me, but she was so mad at me because Drica was pregnant by me. Even if I got down on one knee and proposed, I didn't think she'd say yes.

"Aye, you listening to me boy?"

"Yea, I hear you."

"And when you talk to Keisha, you let her know that Drica ain't getting no abortion! I don't give a shit if you have to tell her that you spoke to me and I forbid it. Let her know what the deal is. She can either accept it and stay with you, or end things for good. Either way, as long as you're being honest with her, shit should work out for the best," Pops said.

While I appreciated the advice my pops was giving me, there was no way that I was going to tell Keisha anything about Drica keeping the baby. The last thing I wanted was for us to continue arguing about that. Nothing was going to change the fact that Drica was pregnant with my kid. No amount of prayers on Keisha's part was going to change that. Drica was going to have my baby and there was nothing Keisha or anyone else could do about it.

"Can you and ma watch the kids for me one more night? I just gotta try and make things right with Keisha," I said.

"Damn. Another night with all that whoopin' and hollerin'. I'm need to get drunk on their lil asses," my pops said. I knew he was just joking though. He and my mom loved watching the kids.

"Uh huh, whatever Pops!" I said with a laugh.

I just had to get Keisha to see things from my point of view. We just were going to have to find a way to coexist and get along because my kids with Keisha and my child with Drica were related. Nothing anyone said or did would change the situation I had put us all in. *Lord, what have I gotten myself into?*

CHAPTER THIRTEEN

Keisha

Marcus didn't come home until the next afternoon. I hoped he had some good news for me because if he didn't tell me what I wanted to hear, I was done. I couldn't keep playing these games with Marcus just because I loved him. I wanted to be with him, but I didn't want him to continue being unfaithful to me. My mom always said that if you allowed a man to mistreat and abuse your love, he would keep doing it. You had to figure out your worth and make him realize you were worthy of his love. If he couldn't love you and only you, you had to let him go.

I was going to tell Marcus that. If he didn't and couldn't love me and me alone, I couldn't continue in this relationship.

"Hey babe," he greeted.

"Hey."

"Are you feeling better? Have you calmed down?"

I couldn't believe he was asking me that. I turned to face him with one hand propped on my hip. "I'm as calm as I need to be right now. Let's talk about where you've been all night and morning," I said.

"Well, I just came from my parents' place. I had a long talk with my Pops. He said to tell you hello," he said.

I knew that was a lie because his dad couldn't stand me. He thought I was some evil bitch that trapped his son into being with her. I didn't trap Marcus, nor did I force him to stay with me. When I told him that I was pregnant in my junior year, he felt obligated to stay with me. He did tell me that he loved me, so I was sure that was the real reason. The fact that I had gotten pregnant again before we even graduated threw our plans off, but it wasn't my fault.

When I told Marcus that I was pregnant the second time, I let him know straight up that I wasn't aborting this baby. I was lucky that the abortion I had four years earlier hadn't left me barren and unable to conceive again. I wouldn't have known what to do with myself if I couldn't have any more kids. What was a woman's purpose in the world if she couldn't even give birth?

"Yea right! Your dad doesn't even like me. Why the hell would he say hello?"

"Well, like I said, we had a long talk and I told him that you were the woman I wanted to be with. I told him that one day, we'd be married so he needed to make more of an effort to get to know you better," he said.

"Oh, please Marcus. We've been together for 15 plus years. Your dad ain't about to get to know me now. He still thinks I'm the reason you gave up your dreams to be a pro ball player," I said.

Marcus used to be a great basketball player in high school. He started playing since we were in elementary and eventually led our high school to the state championship. He was great then and he was even better now, but he chose me and our family instead of the NBA and his dad hated me ever since. I was proud of Marcus for choosing to be a family man instead of some ball player with groupies.

"Well, even though that's true, he still agreed to make amends with you. I know my dad hasn't always been the easiest person to get along with, but I think the two of you should at least try to make this work." He walked over to me and put his arms around my waist. "I love you babe and he understands that. You're an important part of me and his grandkids' lives."

"Whatever! Where are my kids?" I asked as I crossed my arms over my chest.

"Huh? Don't you mean our kids?" He smirked.

"Your kids, my kids, our kids... where the hell are they if you just came from your parents' place?"

"Uh, I asked Pops if they could keep them for one more night," he said with an impish grin on his face.

"What? Why'd you do that?"

"Because baby, the two of us need to make things right between us. I don't want our kids being tossed in the middle of all our damn drama..."

"You mean all your damn drama! All this shit happening between us right now is because of you, not me!" I said. "Own yo shit, Marcus!"

"I am owning my shit! I know I fucked up and I'm sorry about that!"

"Sorry? You're sorry?"

"Yes, I'm sorry."

"So, tell me this... if you're so sorry, did you tell that bitch that she had to get rid of that her little bastard baby?"

I watched as his face twisted up from hearing the word bastard. Marcus hated when I used that word because he thought all kids were blessings. However, if he wanted to keep our relationship intact, he had better get that bitch to get rid of that bastard she was carrying.

"Now, you know I don't like when you use that term."

"Does it look like I give two shits right now? Did you or did you not talk her into getting that abortion? And please don't lie to me

BITTER BABY MAMA'S CLUB

because the streets be talking like crazy, especially if it's about some mess," I said. People could be so fucking messy, especially about my relationship with Marcus.

My friend Fantasia and that bitch's friend Mai, Kai, or something like that… they were two of the messiest bitches in our hood. If you wanted to know anything about anybody, all you had to do was ask those two bitches. They knew the 411 on everybody. So, if Marcus hadn't talked that bitch into doing the right thing, I'd eventually find out about it and it wouldn't be pretty for anyone.

"Yea, I had the talk with her…" Before he could finish his sentence, I busted up in there. I just had to know what she was going to do because what she did would determine the status of my relationship.

"And?"

"And she agreed to go to the clinic and terminate the pregnancy."

"Fa real?"

"Yea, she said she would make an appointment as soon as possible. I even gave her $500 to get it done," he said.

"So, she's gonna get it done?"

"Yep."

I couldn't believe she would just agree to have the abortion without putting up more of an argument. "Did she give you a hard time about doing that?" I asked.

"Well, of course, she argued some. She was pissed that I asked her to 'kill our baby', but I told her that's what had to happen for me to continue to be a part of her life," he said.

I backed out of his embrace. "So, you're gonna keep fucking her?"

94 | P a g e

"No, that's not even the case. I had to tell her that to get her to do what I need her to do."

"Marcus, you'd better not be playing me…" I said as I stared at him with a perplexed expression on my face.

"Babe, I'm not. I love you and I wanna be with you. Once Drica takes care of her lil situation, we can move on and things will go back to the way they used to be."

"Until the next time you fuck with her."

"Ain't gon' be no next time."

"Boy bye! How many times have I heard that before? Shit, I thought you had stopped messing with her until I found out y'all was at the cabin together. I just don't get why you keep doing the same damn thing over and over again. Am I not enough woman for you?" I asked.

"You're more than enough woman for me babe. I don't know why I do the things that I do. I wish I had a better answer for you, but I don't. I can tell you that you're the only woman I wanna be with. And that you're the only woman I can see myself with for the rest of my life," he said with a smile as he reached for me again.

"Please don't do me like you do her…"

"Whatchu mean by that?"

"I don't want you to tell me the shit you think that I wanna hear just to appease me. Tell me the real Marcus. Did you really ask her to get rid of that baby?" I asked.

"I did. Why don't you believe me?"

"Because you've lied to me so many times in the past. How can I trust and believe what you're telling me now?"

He lifted my chin with his forefinger, forcing me to stare in his eyes. "Do you still love me Keisha?"

"Of course, I still love you. If I didn't still love you, I would've been gone a long time ago," I admitted. No matter what Marcus did to me, my heart continued to beat to the same rhythm as his. I loved that man to my soul and even though I had tried on many occasions to hate him and walk away, I couldn't. I couldn't deprive my kids of their father. I couldn't deprive them of growing up in a two-parent household. If I did that, then I would be labeled the bad guy in this situation. For the sake of my family and my kids, I had to do my best to make this work... by any means necessary.

"And I love you babe. You've had my heart for the longest time and I don't see that changing any time soon," he said as he leaned his head for a kiss. As much as I wanted to turn my head the other way, the truth of the matter is I wanted him to kiss me. Marcus was my man and I knew that if I turned him away, there was another bitch waiting to scoop him right up.

So, what did I do? I puckered and allowed him to thrust his hot tongue inside my mouth. As the kiss grew more heated, all thoughts of Drica and her little bastard disappeared from my mind. The only thing I was concerned about right now was pleasing my man. As he gripped my firm, plump ass cheeks in his hands, he tongued me down like there was no tomorrow. A moan escaped my lips as he pressed me up against the wall. His lips traveled to my neck where his tongue ran in circles.

"Mmmm," I moaned as his right hand traveled inside my pants and panties. As he toyed with my kitty cat, I could feel myself reaching climactic pleasure. He removed his hand and led me to the bedroom. I followed behind him ready to make it do what it do.

He laid me on the bed and pulled my pants and panties off. He threw the clothing to the side and began to lick my thighs, causing fireworks to explode inside my belly. This was how I knew that I was deeply in love with Marcus. He literally gave me chills and fireworks. As his tongue traveled to my most precious and sensitive spot, I braced myself for what was to come. He slid his tongue inside my moistened crevice and began to suck on my pearl.

"Sssss!" I hissed as he drove his tongue deeper inside me. My legs were shaking like crazy from the amazing sensations this man sent coursing through my body. As my juices came to the surface, he slurped it all up. He stood up and removed his bottoms and t-shirt as I tossed my shirt to the side as well.

He climbed in bed and hovered over me as he inserted himself inside me. I gasped and gripped the bed sheets as he pummeled inside me over and over again, hitting my G-spot every single time. "Oh shit!" I crooned. "I'm about to cum!"

"Cum on daddy dick, baby!"

Fucking right I was gonna cum on his dick. If I played my cards right, I'd cum on it more than once tonight. I raked my nails over his back as I released once again. By the time we were done, I was feeling much better about our relationship and where we were headed. I just hoped that Marcus wouldn't let me down again. I didn't know if my heart could take another let down.

"I love you babe," he whispered as I laid in his arms.

"I love you too."

He held me close as we got ready to go to sleep. *God if you're listening, please don't let us fall off. I love this man so much, but if he falls back into his old habits again, give me the strength to walk away.*

That was my prayer that I made before I closed my eyes.

CHAPTER FOURTEEN

Drica

Six weeks later...

Please tell me why Marcus had promised me that we'd be a family if he didn't mean it. Now that I was having a baby, everything made me emotional. Why the hell did pregnant women have to be so damn sensitive? It seemed as if I cried for everything. Especially now that Marcus wouldn't sleep with me. I needed dick now more than ever before because not only was this pregnancy making me emotional, but it was also making me horny.

If I could spend my days in bed having sex with Marcus, that would be fine with me. However, it had been six damn weeks since the last time we made love. He came by to see me and even came with me to my last doctor's appointment. But he left my house before we could get it on.

No matter how much I tried to get him to give me some, he wouldn't. Hell, he wouldn't even let me suck his dick to get him started.

"What's the problem?"

"There is no problem," he said.

"That's a lie! You always ready for sex."

"Well, I ain't ready right now. I just went with you for your doctor's appointment and now I'm going home," he said.

"I thought you said if I'd keep the baby that things between us would be different."

"It is different."

"Yea, different in the worse way. I mean, I can't even get no dick from you. Hell, I might as well start looking for another man if you won't give me any," I said.

"I'll be damn if you gon' be fucking some other nigga with my baby in yo stomach. You ain't finna have no other nigga's nut on my baby head!"

"You have no say in what I do. If you won't fuck me, someone else will."

Of course, I was making an idle threat. I wasn't trying to sleep with no one else, especially since I was four months along. I didn't want some other dude giving me what I craved. I wanted my baby daddy to put it on me the way that he used to, but how long did he expect me to wait for the D? I had needs just like any other pregnant female. Shit, I craved sex more now than I did before I got pregnant.

"I bet not."

"I bet he will," I said as I crossed my arms over my chest.

"Drica I'm not playing with you. If I find out you giving my goodies to some other nigga..."

"What? What are you going to do about it? And these aren't your goodies anymore, they're mine to do with whatever the hell I want to. You ever heard that saying, 'What one chick won't do another one will'? Well, the same goes for niggas. What one nigga won't do another one will. I'm tired of sitting around waiting for you to do the right thing by me. If you don't want me, I'll find someone who does," I said.

He could pretend that what I was saying wasn't bothering him, but I could tell that it was. The look on his face remained unbothered, but the twitch to the side of his mouth spoke volumes. Every time he was bothered by something, his mouth twitched.

"Alright, if you fuck with some other nigga, have him take you to your doctor's appointments!"

"What?"

"You heard what the fuck I said. If you wanna give him the pussy, have him go with you to your doctor's appointments."

"But this is your baby! What nigga is gonna wanna attend doctor's appointments with me for your kid?"

"I don't know, but it won't be this nigga."

"That's not fair. How can you not fuck me, but don't want me to sleep with anyone else? I'm only four months along, which means I have five months to go plus the down time for me to recover."

"And?"

"So, you expect me to wait seven months to get some dick?" I was so confused by his attitude. I thought men loved pregnant pussy. I thought he said that things would be the same. I mean, not the same because I wanted him to be with me and not Keisha, but what was I gonna do now?

"Look, I'm just telling you how it's gonna be. If you want me to be a part of this kid's life, you better not have no other nigga nutting on that kid's head!" He was so pissed, but hell, so was I. What kind of shit was that?

That was six weeks ago, and I had been craving sex ever since. Today, me and my cousin London were going baby shopping. I wanted to have a baby shower and a gender reveal party, but I didn't think that Marcus would attend. I was ready and waiting for London by 11:30 that morning. By noon, she still hadn't gotten here. I wondered what the hell happened to her. I pulled out my phone and called her.

She answered on the third ring. "I'm on my way!"

"I thought you were coming get me at 11:30," I said.

"I had something unexpected come up, but I'm on my way now."

"You alright? You sound a little rattled."

"I'm fine. I'll talk to you when I get there."

"Okay."

She ended the call before I could say anything else. I hoped that things with her were okay. I knew that she had been having problems with Shane ever since she told him she was pregnant. That was something we definitely had in common. We both had been trying to train our dogs since informing them that we were pregnant, but they weren't having it. I wondered did all pregnant women go through this shit with their men.

CHAPTER FIFTEEN

Marcus

As tired as I was, I didn't feel like doing nothing today. But unfortunately, doing nothing wasn't an option. Today was the day that Drica was going to the doctor for one of her prenatal checkups. Since I hadn't been around much lately, she demanded that I go with her to this one. I thought about telling her that I wouldn't be able to make it, but I knew that would only stress her out, which wouldn't be healthy for the baby.

Only problem was that Keisha was home today. With her being a makeup artist, she didn't have a set schedule. She basically worked when she felt like it or when she got booked, which was every couple of days lately. I guess that was her way of sticking around to watch how I moved.

"Good morning, bae. What you doing up so early?" She asked as she walked out of the bathroom wrapped in a towel with her toothbrush dangling from her mouth.

"Good morning. I got a couple runs to make today," I replied.

She raised her right eyebrow and pulled the toothbrush out of her mouth, then smirked.

"Runs? What kind of runs? And since when do you do anything during the week?"

"Since business calls. I ain't gon' be long though. Just for a few hours."

"Well since you won't be long, I'm coming with you," she replied. "I already took my shower, so it won't take long for me to get dressed and do my hair."

I laughed and shook my head.

"Nah, as much as I would like for you to come, that won't be necessary. This something I gotta do alone."

"Marcus why?" she pouted. "I always go with you, so what makes this time so different?"

"Cuz man. I don't want you around none of that shit no more. Just chill at the crib and wait for me to come back. Besides, if you come with me, I don't know if I'll be finished in time for you to pick up the kids from school."

"But you said you'd only be gone for a few hours. It's just 9:00am."

"I know what I said, but the answer is still no."

Without responding, she rolled her eyes and stormed off back into the bathroom. I wasn't tryna upset her, but ain't no way in hell was I about to let her come with me. She would lose her shit if I pulled up to Drica's house to take her to the doctor after I lied and told her that she got an abortion. I still hadn't found a way to tell Keisha that Drica was keeping the baby, and to be honest, I didn't know when or if I would tell her at all. Drica was only five months, so I still had time, but I was content with not having to hear no shit from Keisha for the next four months or so.

After I got myself together, I ran downstairs and shot Drica a text to let her know that I would soon be on my way. But just as I was about to walk out, Keisha walked up on me with her arms folded and her bottom lip poked out.

"What's wrong with you?" I asked her as I grabbed my keys off the counter.

"So, you really not gon' take me with you?"

"Keisha don't do this right now. We been doing good and ain't been having no arguments. I'd like to keep it that way."

"You're still seeing her, aren't you?"

"What? Seeing who? What the fuck you talking about?"

"You know exactly who I'm talking about."

"Yo' you buggin'," I replied while shaking my head. "I'll hit you up when I'm on my way back."

She ran to the front door and threw herself across the threshold, blocking it.

"You're still seeing Drica, huh? Just tell me the truth."

"Come on man! I'm telling you the fucking truth Keisha! I ain't seeing nobody but your crazy ass! Now move! I got somewhere to be!"

"Then why the fuck can't I go with you? Just answer that and I'll move out of your way."

"So, you really gon' assume that I'm still fucking with the girl just cuz you can't come with me to make a run? You know how stupid you sound right now bruh! You told me to tell her to get a fucking abortion, and I did that! It ain't been shit between us ever since! Shit, that girl don't even want nothing to do with me because I chose you over her!"

"Put that on our kids."

"What? Man, fuck no! I ain't putting shit on my children! Either you believe me, or you don't, but don't drag my kids into your bullshit!"

"Nigga you've been lying to me so much, it's hard to believe anything that comes out of your mouth!"

"Then don't! You ain't gotta believe shit if you don't want to! But if you still can't trust me after I did everything you asked me to do, then all this shit is pointless!"

"So, what are you implying?" She asked.

"I'm saying, if you ain't happy, my nigga then leave! If you don't trust me, then we obviously don't need to be together! Cuz I ain't gon' keep letting you accuse me of shit I know I ain't doing! Matter of fact…"

I grabbed her arm and pushed her out of the way, then walked out the house and slammed the door. Even though I was lying, she ain't had no reason to come at me about no shit with Drica. The two of them hadn't seen or heard from each other in months, so all that bullshit was uncalled for. But since she didn't trust me, then she could leave. At this point, I no longer gave a fuck.

When I finally got to Drica's apartment complex, I sent her a text and waited for her to come out. Usually, I'd go up there and help her come down, but after that shit with Keisha I just wasn't feeling it right now. A couple of minutes later, she came flying around the corner dressed in a Nike sweat suit with her hair tied up.

"Hey baby," she said as she slid in the car.

"What's up?" I answered dryly.

She smacked her lips and fastened her seatbelt then turned to me.

"Wow, what's up? No hey bae, I miss you, or nothing? Just that ol' dry ass what's up?"

"Drica…"

"Alright Marcus," she said as she waved her hands in there. "I guess Keisha pissed you off or something, so now you're gonna take it out on me. Fine, I get it."

"I ain't taking nothing out on you. I'm just not in a good head space right now."

"I don't know why. Today is the day we find out what we're having, so if anything, you should be just as happy as I am."

"I am happy, and you know that."

"I sure can't tell."

"What you want me to do Drica?" I asked irritatingly. "You want me to jump for joy or shout it out to the world?"

"No. I'm just saying..."

Before she could finish her sentence, I let down the driver's side window and stuck my neck out.

"Today is the day I find out what my girl is having y'all! I'm so excited I just couldn't keep it to myself!"

"Marcus, are you serious?"

"What? That's what you wanted, huh?" I asked as I let the window back up.

"It's not that serious though."

"My point exactly."

"What the fuck is your problem? Every time that bitch make you mad, you start trippin' out and shit. That's not fair."

"I ain't trippin Drica. A nigga just stressed out."

"And you don't think I am? I'm pregnant with your baby, but it's like I'm going through it alone."

"But you not."

"That's what it feels like. I have to schedule appointments just to see you. I can only call you at certain times. You barely come over anymore. I'm starting to think that if it wasn't for the baby, you wouldn't want anything to do with me."

"That ain't true, so don't even try to pull that card on me. You knew what time it was when we got together. I told you I had a girl, and what did you say?"

She looked out of the window without responding.

"Don't turn your head now. What you said? Or you forgot? Cuz if you forgot, I can remind you."

"What I said doesn't matter now Marcus. The point is, we BOTH put ourselves in this situation. Just like I knew you had a girl, so did you. But that didn't stop you from fucking me and getting me pregnant, so it shouldn't stop you from being there for me when I need you the most. This is my first pregnancy, and it's really not fair to me or our child that you're not always available for us."

"Drica when you call, I always come running. I'm here now, ain't I?"

"Yes! Now you are! But once we leave the doctor's office, it'll be like I don't exist!"

"Look, I'm trying alright. This shit ain't easy for me either. To be honest, I got a lot more on my shoulders than you think I do."

"Like what?" She asked as she crossed her arms over her chest with a smirk on her face.

"Like having to keep you and Keisha both satisfied and separated from each other. You don't think that's stressful for me? Yea, you and I agreed to fuck around, but she didn't ask to be part of our shit. But I made her part of it when I laid down with you, so now I gotta deal with it. You don't."

"What's her issue anyway? I mean, does she not accept our baby or something?"

"It ain't that she don't accept it. She just having a hard time trying to adjust to the situation."

"Well, I hope she comes around sooner rather than later, cuz this baby is here to stay and will be part of both of your lives whether she likes it or not."

I nodded my head and continued to drive. I didn't know how to respond to her, so I figured it was best that I didn't say shit. At the end of the day, I had no one to blame for my stress but myself. But that still didn't stop me from feeling bad for Drica. Here she was thinking we were about to be just one big happy family, when in reality we wouldn't be close to that. If only she knew how Keisha really felt.

CHAPTER SIXTEEN

Drica

I had hoped that once Marcus found out that I was actually pregnant, things between us would go better than they had been. I thought once Keisha knew bout our baby, she'd know that she had to split her time with Marcus. I didn't think Keisha would continue to try and keep Marcus away from me. What woman in her right mind would try to keep a man from being a part of his baby's life? I was glad that he had put his foot down and came to get me to take me to my doctor's appointment because I didn't want to go by myself.

If only Marcus understood how much I loved him. I had been defending him and our relationship ever since we got together. I was tired of doing that, but my love for him made me do it. He drove the rest of the way to the doctor's office in silence. I was cool with that though because my only concern right now was finding out the sex of our baby. I couldn't wait to find out if I was having a boy or girl.

We walked in the office hand in hand. If he thought I wasn't going to hold his hand, he had another thought coming. I wanted any and everybody to know that my baby daddy was here with me and that we were still together. I walked up to the receptionist's desk to sign in while Marcus took a seat in the waiting room. I glanced over at him and caught him on his phone, fingers tapping like crazy. I wondered who the hell he was texting even though I already knew who it was.

I knew that Keisha was probably giving him grief about coming with me to the doctor's, but he was my child's father too. He owed me just as much time as he had given her when she was pregnant... all three times. As I made my way over to where Marcus was sitting, he stuffed his phone in his pocket. I sat down and looked over at him.

"What?" He asked as he glanced at me.

"Who were you texting... Keisha?" I asked.

"Nah, I was checking IG."

"Oh, were you posting your whereabouts? Were you letting your followers know you were with your baby mama at the doctor?" I smirked.

"No, that ain't nobody's business but our own."

"I'm sure gonna post that shit!" I said as I grabbed my phone.

He placed his hand over my phone screen, causing me to stare at him with my mouth wide open. "Don't do that!"

"Don't do that? Why not?" I asked. "Just because you don't want to talk about what's going on with you that doesn't mean I don't want my friends to know that I'm about to have my first ultrasound for my first child. Why wouldn't I be happy about that?"

"I never said you couldn't be happy about it Drica. You putting words in my mouth. I only said that's our business, not anyone else's."

"Are you serious right now? I told you that's my first baby." Something about his attitude didn't seem right. "Are you sure Keisha knows you're here with me?"

"Hell yea, she knows! That's why I don't need you putting that shit all over social media! You know that the two of us are still together. You posting that shit is gon' make her feel like you mocking her or something," he said in a harsh whisper.

"Damn Marcus. I sure can't wait til you care about me that much," I said.

"I do care about you Drica. I'm here, ain't I?" He asked with a slight attitude.

"I guess."

"Cedrica!" The nurse called my name. The two of us stood up and made our way to the back. I saw this chick sitting in a corner staring at me like she knew me and wondered if we had met somewhere before. I guess Marcus didn't notice her because he didn't say anything. We followed the nurse to the check-up area, so she could check my temp, blood pressure, weight, and pulse.

As I stood on the scale, I watched the scale wobble until she came to 143 pounds. "143 pounds!!" I cried. Shit, just last month I was 135. Now, she was telling me that I had gained eight pounds in a month.

"Yep, you might wanna watch that because you don't wanna gain too much weight during your pregnancy. It'll definitely be harder to take off than to put on," Tamara advised.

"How much weight gain is normal during pregnancy?" I asked. I was proud of my shape. I had a plump ass, thick thighs, and before I got pregnant, I only had a little fluff around my midsection. I didn't wanna gain too much weight and be floppy.

"Well, a pregnant woman typically gains between three to four pounds in the first trimester. Then you have the second and third trimester where the average pregnant woman typically gains four pounds a month."

"She gained eight pounds since last month, so what does that mean?" Marcus asked.

Well, look at his ass asking questions about my weight gain and shit. I smiled because my baby daddy must really care about me to be asking questions about me. "It doesn't necessarily mean anything, except that she gained a few more pounds than the average."

"So, her blood pressure and everything is okay?" Marcus asked.

"Yea, she's fine. Follow me," the nurse said as she led us to an exam room.

Once inside the exam room, I sat down on the table and Marcus sat in the chair next to me. Ten minutes later, Dr. Ellis walked in and began asking me questions. "Hello you two, how are y'all doing today?"

"I'm fine Dr. Ellis."

"I'm straight," Marcus mumbled.

"So, I see you gained a little more weight than I expected you too. Your blood pressure is slightly elevated…"

"Am I gonna have a high risk pregnancy? Does that mean I need medication? Is my baby okay?" I just fired question after question at her without giving her a chance to respond.

"Calm down. I did say your BP was slightly elevated, so there's no need to put you on medication. It isn't high enough for that. It's too soon to say whether your pregnancy will be high risk or not. You should be okay, but if you have some extra stress in your life, you should always try to remain calm. Stress is never good for you or your baby. The less stress you have in your life, the better off you and your baby will be."

As she was talking, I turned my attention to Marcus to make sure that he was paying attention to what the doctor was saying. I needed to have as little stress as possible, so I could have a safe pregnancy and healthy baby. "Let's get your ultrasound done," Dr. Ellis said.

I lifted my shirt as she placed the paper sheet over the waistband of my pants. She squirted some warm gel on my belly and rolled the small white wand on it. Marcus and I watched as a picture of our little baby popped up on the screen. I stuck my hand out to Marcus and he took it and held it tight. "Is the baby okay?" I asked.

"She's fine. See that right there? That's her heartbeat. Would y'all like to hear it?" Dr. Ellis asked.

"Oh my God! Yes please!" I said. I couldn't contain my excitement as the tears flooded my eyes. Marcus smiled at me and I could tell he was equally excited. No matter how Keisha felt about me, Marcus was just as much an important part of my life as he was hers. She was just going to have to accept our baby as a part of her life because her children are related to my baby no matter how she felt about it.

The doctor turned up the volume on the monitor and I could hear my little one's heart beating strong through the speakers. "Wow! Her heartbeat sounds so strong!" I said full of happiness. My heart was overflowing with so much love for my precious baby. It didn't even matter to me if it was a boy or girl because I was going to love and protect my baby forever.

"It is strong. Did you all wanna know the sex of the baby today?" Dr. Ellis asked.

I looked over at Marcus and he asked, "You wanna know?"

"You know I wanna know," I said.

He looked back at the doctor and said, "Sure."

She rolled the wand over my stomach some more and smiled at us. "You're having a little girl!"

"A little girl? Really?" I asked. I was super excited that I was having a girl. I couldn't wait to buy her all kinds of pretty pink clothes and decorate a nursery for her. I lived in a one- bedroom apartment and had been trying to get Marcus to help me with a two bedroom. He seemed to think that I didn't need more than one bedroom. He said since I was from the projects, I should be used to living in a cramped space. I didn't find that shit was funny at all.

"Yes, that's her little arm right there. She's actually sucking her thumb right now," Dr. Ellis said.

"Awww! I can't wait to meet her," I gushed. "Babe, we're having a little girl!"

"I know. Another girl," he said with a smile.

"Oh, I thought you said this was your first baby," Dr. Ellis said as she glanced at me.

"Oh, she is, but my boo has three other children with his other baby mama."

Humph! *That was embarrassing.*

"Oh okay. Well, blended families can be pretty cool. Your baby will already have siblings to play with," she said.

If she only knew. I knew by Marcus' attitude when he picked me up earlier that Keisha was having a hard time accepting the fact that I was pregnant. I wish she'd get over all her anger toward me. I didn't think that we'd ever be friends, but I think if she'd just accept the things she couldn't change, we could co-exist pretty good. But I wasn't about to kiss her ass though. I mean, she might have been in Marcus' life first, but I was a part of his life now and we were having a baby too.

I didn't even respond to Dr. Ellis when she said that because I knew getting Keisha to accept my baby girl would be like pulling teeth from a four-year old. I just smiled and continued to look at the monitor because my baby was still on it. I watched as she took measurements before printing pictures of the ultrasound. She wiped the gel from my belly and removed the paper towel and threw it in the trash. She handed the pictures to me and smiled.

"Your baby girl is growing fabulously and she's healthy. I'd like to see you again a month from now and hopefully, your blood pressure won't be elevated. I'm going to need you to keep her as stress free as possible sir," she said to Marcus.

He smiled and said, "I'll do my best."

The fact that he was sitting here with me meant a lot to me. However, he wasn't off the hook yet. I mean, he was just as much a parent to our child as I was. The doctor addressed him to keep me stress free, but he was the bulk of where my stress came from. All I wanted was for the two of us to be together. I wished I could get him to forget about Keisha. That bitch wasn't worried about me, so why should I be worried about her?

As Marcus and I made our way to the receptionist's desk to check out and get my next appointment, I held his hand. He looked down at me and asked, "You happy now?"

"You have no idea! We're having a girl!" I said as I smiled from ear to ear.

"Yea, I know."

"Can we go to Target and pick up a few things for her?" I asked. Something about the look on his face told me he was about to say no. "Pleeeeeease baby. Our baby is going to need a lot of stuff. We may as well start shopping early."

He ran his hand down his face before looking at me. "Babe please!"

"Aight," he finally relented. I was so happy that I flung my arms around him and gave him a huge kiss on the lips. It didn't matter to me who was watching. I just loved this man so much. I got my appointment card and we walked out of the doctor's office hand in hand.

The girl that was sitting in the corner when we were on our way to the back area was still there. It looked like she was on the phone with someone, but her eyes were still on me and Marcus. Who the hell was she and why was she watching us like that? She was lucky that I was in a good mood and pregnant because babeeeee, if I wasn't…

CHAPTER SEVENTEEN

Keisha

I couldn't even lie. I was feeling bummed out that Marcus didn't let me go with him. I thought that would've been a good time for us to spend some quality time together. I also loved to travel, so anytime I could take that trip with him, I didn't hesitate. I mean, I didn't have any clients coming so my schedule was free. I just didn't know why he wouldn't let me come. He had better not be hiding nothing from me.

As much as I tried and wanted to trust Marcus, his past spoke volumes and prevented me from doing that. It was like no matter how much I tried to put my trust in him, that feeling that he was still messing with that project bitch kept nagging at me. To be honest, I didn't even know how their relationship started. I mean, why would he mess with her anyway when he had all of me? I was more than enough to satisfy any man, so Marcus didn't need to cheat on me, but he did.

All that shit he had spat at me about her being just a friend and telling me that I was being silly for my "jealous rants" was a lie. I had every reason to feel the way I felt because the two of them had been sleeping together behind my back. When I found out that bitch had her claws in my man, they had been fucking for almost a year. How could I have been so blind all that time?

When I confronted him about it, of course, he denied it. Eventually, I caught them together thanks to my amazing P.I. skills. He apologized and cried; something he hadn't done since the birth of our first child. Because he cried and swore he wouldn't see her again, I stayed with him. But I was a fool because the relationship continued behind my back until I threw him out. However, throwing him out didn't do shit either because I took him back.

You had to understand how much I loved Marcus. We had been together since I was 13 years old and we were now 28, so you can imagine how much love I felt for that man. My friends told me that I should leave him. Their reasoning was why would I continue to be with a man who kept disrespecting me and I didn't even have a ring to show for it. The truth was I believed that God put Marcus and I together for a reason. He blessed us with three beautiful kids and I couldn't just walk away from the family we had built.

It was true that he hadn't popped the question yet, but I believe one day he would. I couldn't wait either because I'd say yes. I mean, he had that little bitch get an abortion for me when I knew he didn't believe in that shit. It took a while for me to understand his feelings about abortion because he definitely didn't express the same feelings for me when we were younger. But he was right at the end of the day because we were too young to have a child. We were kids ourselves and our parents would've freaked out big time.

Even though I went on to have three other children, I'd never forget the baby that I gave up. I don't think women ever forget something like that. It was a horrible time for me, but Marcus was so supportive. I mean, he came by to check on me that whole weekend. I didn't have any down time because my mom didn't know what I had done. She always made sure I took my ass to school every damn day. So, two days after my "procedure," I was back in school cramps and all.

Let me stop talking about that because it always managed to bring a tear or two to my eyes. I continued to clean house until my phone started ringing. I went to the kitchen counter to pick it up. I didn't recognize the number, but I picked up anyway. I mean, what if it was the police calling about Marcus being in an accident.

"Hello."

"Hey girl," came the female voice on the other end of the line.

"Who is this?"

"It's Shayla."

"Shayla? Lena's friend?" I asked.

I didn't know why she was calling me. It had me wondering if something happened to my little sister.

"Yes girl," she said as if we were best friends or something.

"What can I do for you Shayla? Did something happen to Lena?"

"Shit, I don't know. Ain't she your sister?" She said with a slight attitude.

"Why are you calling me then? How did you get my number anyway?"

"Lena gave it to me... DUH!! Anyway, I was calling to give you the tea about yo baby daddy, but if you don't want it…"

What the fuck was she talking about? Where did she see Marcus at?

"What are you talking about Shayla? Marcus is out of town!" I said.

"Out of town? Is that what he told you?"

"Look lil' girl, I don't have time to play games with you. Say what you need to say because I got shit to do!"

"Well damn! You ain't gotta get no attitude with me. I'm trying to help you out!"

"Just say it girl... damn!!"

"Okay, I was sitting at my doctor's office for my appointment cuz you know I'm pregnant, right?"

Who the fuck cared if she was pregnant or not? I mean, she wasn't having my fucking baby, was she? Why the hell she telling me all this bullshit about her at the doctor's office?

"Get to the point!"

"Well, I was sitting there waiting for my name to be called when your man walked in with Drica..."

"DRICA?"

"Yea, his other bitch! They're at my doctor's office right now," she said.

"Girl, quit playing!"

"Why would I call you and tell you that if it wasn't the truth? I ain't got no reason to lie to you!"

How could Marcus be at the doctor's office with Drica? Why were they at the obstetrician's office anyway? I thought he had told her to have an abortion. I thought he said she wasn't pregnant anymore.

"What doctor's office are you at?" I asked.

"The women's clinic on South Parkway," Shayla said before I hung the phone up.

I quickly stuffed my feet in my flip flops and grabbed my purse and keys before rushing out the door. I looked up the address on my phone and saw that I was 20 minutes away. I jumped in my car and hopped on the highway, speeding to get there so I could catch Marcus in the act. If he was over there with Drica, I was going to bust him in the head until his white meat spilled all over the sidewalk.

I finally made it there and rushed in the office. I looked all around but didn't see Marcus or Drica's ugly ass anywhere. I made my way to the receptionist's desk.

"Hello, may I help you?"

"Yes, I'm looking for a patient, Cedrica Wallace. Is she here?"

"Who are you?" The girl behind the desk asked.

"A friend. Is she here or not?" I asked.

"I'm sorry ma'am, I can't disclose that information. Our patient info is confidential," she said.

"I'm not asking you to disclose that bitch's information. I'm asking if she's here."

"I can't give you that information either. We have to protect our patients…"

"Protect your patients from what? I'm just asking if the bitch is here or not!!" I was super angry and tired of this bitch. I pulled out my phone and scrolled to a picture of Marcus. "Fine, don't tell me shit about her. Have you seen him here?" I shoved the phone in her face, but she remained tight lipped.

"I'm sorry ma'am, but…"

I turned my attention to the patients waiting to be seen in the waiting room. I turned the picture of Marcus around and shoved it in their faces. "HAS ANYONE SEEN THIS MAN?! WAS HE HERE?!" I yelled. Everyone looked around and at each other, but none of them would look at me. "C'MON, I KNOW SOMEBODY SAW SOMETHING! DID Y'ALL SEE HIM IN HERE WITH SOME OTHER BITCH?!!"

I knew that I looked stupid and desperate, but I needed to know if Marcus had been here. "Ma'am, I'm gonna have to ask you to leave," the receptionist said as she tried to escort me out.

"TAKE YOUR FUCKIN' HANDS OFF ME, BITCH!! WITH THAT BIG ASS GAP AND SHIT! I CAN SEE YOUR FUCKIN' LACE FRONT BITCH!" I shrieked as I shrugged her off.

"If you don't leave, I'll have to contact the police!" She said in a stern tone while she glared at me. She could look all she wanted to, but I bet she wouldn't touch me though. She didn't want these problems, but she could get it through.

"Fine!" I flipped my hair over my shoulder and walked out. As soon as I made it outside, I called Marcus' phone. He didn't answer, so I called again. I hit the call button like four times, but never got a response from him.

His phone continued to go to voicemail every time I called, so I gave up. It was cool because he had to return home sooner or later. I wished Shayla had sent me a picture, so I could've shown to him once he made it back. Without receipts, all I had was her word against his and I knew he would lie his ass off. I mean, what reason would Shayla have to lie to me?

I got back in my car, fuming. I couldn't believe that Marcus had lied to me. As I started my car, my phone rang. It was Marcus. "Hello."

"Hey baby, you called?"

"Yes, why didn't you answer when I called you before?"

"I have my phone on vibrate and I didn't feel it. You know how loud my music can be."

"Uh huh. Marcus where are you?" I asked.

"What? You know where I am. I told you this morning I had a run to make," he said.

"I know but where are you?"

"What's going on babe? Don't tell me you trippin' again," he said.

"Why don't you just answer the question? Where the hell are you?" I asked.

"I'm on my way to Tony's place. What the hell is going on?"

"Did you see Drica today?"

"Did I see who?"

"You heard me nigga! Don't act like you ain't heard me ask you if you saw that bitch!"

"Are you kidding me? You know when I go on these runs I only take you or one of my boys with me!"

"Well, you didn't take me, so who did you take with you?" I asked.

"What?"

"Did I stutter my nigga? Who is with you?"

"Oh, Lucas is with me."

"Lucas with you right now?"

"Yes, where is this shit coming from? I thought we were past all these insecurities babe," he said.

"Really Marcus? I don't know where you got that shit from! Now, lemme holla at Lucas," I said.

"Oh, he ain't in the truck right this minute. He's in the store getting some drinks and paying for gas," he explained.

"So, you've been with Lucas all day?"

"Yea, babe. Can you please tell me what the problem is now?"

"Nothing. Just be careful," I said feeling foolish for bothering him.

"I will. I love you," he said.

"I love you too."

We ended the call and I breathed a sigh of relief. I wondered why Shayla lied to me. Bitches were always trying to come between me and my man. They were nothing but haters trying to get what I had. If I had to listen to every bitch that tried to break up me and Marcus, we wouldn't have made it to 15 years. As long as the two of us had been together, I had to have some level of trust.

Now, I was a little worried about him falling back in Drica's arms, but not too worried. The fact that we had three kids and she had just aborted hers gave me the upper hand. I could keep Marcus in line with our kids because he loved them, and he wanted a family. His dad may not have liked me too much, but he loved his grandkids and he wanted them to have the best life.

He wanted our kids to grow up with a mother and father in the household, so I knew that he would do everything he could to keep me and Marcus together. My kids deserved to have their parents together because I grew up in a household without a father. I wanted more for my kids than what my mom could give her kids.

My mom struggled to raise my siblings and I by herself. It was hard and there were plenty of times we had to get told no. That was the worst part of my childhood; not being able to do what my friends could because we couldn't afford it. I didn't want my kids to have to go through that. My kids were innocent in anything that Marcus and I had going on. Why should they suffer because one of their parents couldn't do right?

That was my main reason for taking all that shit I had been dealing with from Marcus. I knew that people were talking about me behind my back, but I didn't care. I wanted my kids to have a family with two parents in the same house. No one understood my reasons for staying with my man even though he openly cheated on me, but I didn't need them to understand. I knew, and I understood it, so that was all that mattered.

Marcus and I had been through a lot together. God always gave people trials and tribulations to go through to see how strong they are. I thought I had proven my strength a long time ago, but I was still going through it. I was going to do what I had to do to keep my man because the alternative was nothing nice. I made it back home and went about my business, cleaning up my house before it was time to go get the kids from school.

Please let Marcus be telling the truth about his whereabouts because I didn't think I'd be able to hand another betrayal.

CHAPTER EIGHTEEN

Marcus

I wondered why Keisha kept blowing my damn phone up. Like, I couldn't just answer her with Drica right there because I knew Drica would start running her mouth. Keisha didn't even know that I was with her right now and I wasn't about to let her find out this way. As we looked through the baby clothes in Target, I decided to send her to the dressing room, so I could call Keisha back. I knew if I didn't call her back, I'd have hell to pay when I got home.

"How about we got to the maternity section and pick out a couple of things for you to try on?" I suggested.

"Really baby?"

"Yea, I love to see a woman in maternity clothes," I said with a big smile.

"Aww, thanks babe," she said as she grabbed me by the hand and led me to that department. As she browsed through the clothes, my phone continued to vibrate in my pocket. She finally found a couple of dresses and some shorts she wanted to try on. She went inside the dressing room while I waited.

I pulled my phone out and hurriedly dialed Keisha's number. She sounded upset and out of breath as she started questioning my whereabouts. Like, why was she asking me where I was when she knew where I was supposed to be. Of course, I had to lie through my teeth and I hoped she would believe me, so I could be off the phone by the time Drica came out. No such luck. Drica emerged from the dressing room and saw me on the phone.

I hurried to get Keisha on the phone before Drica made her way over to where I stood. I was finally able to hang the phone up just in time for Drica to stand by me with the pouty mouth. "Why yo face look like that?" I asked.

"Who were you on the phone with?"

"Lucas, why? You wanted to talk to him or something?" I asked.

"No, I was just curious."

"Don't be questioning me about who I'm on the phone with though. That shit ain't cool when I pay my own phone bill. When you decide you wanna pay my bill, I'll gladly tell you who I'm talking to," I said.

"Well damn. You ain't gotta catch no attitude!"

"I ain't got no attitude. I'm just tired of y'all questioning me about my damn business like I ain't a man and can't take care of my damn self!" I said.

"Well, that quickly went left."

"Yea, it did. The outfit is cute by the way."

"Thanks," she said as she made her way back to the dressing room. I knew she was feeling some kind of way, but I didn't care. I was tired of these women coming at me like I had to answer to their asses.

I was a grown ass man and not one of them paid my damn bills, so neither of them had any rights to ask me anything. Drica came out of the dressing room with a disappointed look on her face. I knew she wanted me to baby her ass, but I wasn't going to do it. She was having a baby, so she needed to act like it and grow the hell up. How she expected to be able to take care of a newborn when she kept acting like one?

"You got the shit you wanna buy?" I asked her.

"I don't want anything. My mood has been shot to shit…"

"Say no mo'. Let's go," I said as I led the way out of the store.

I wasn't about to beg her to buy shit. She wanted to act like a child, then I'd treat her just like a child. She followed behind me sulking just like a child. Once we got in the truck, I asked, "What's your damn problem Drica?"

"I didn't like how you spoke to me in front of those people in the store," she said.

"In front of what people girl? Ain't nobody was looking at you!"

"You still spoke to me like shit!"

"Look Drica, I said what I said and that's it. You need to grow up. In a few months, you gon' be a mama with a newborn to raise. So, you may as well start practicing being grown now…"

"Start practicing? What you mean by that?" She asked looking offended.

"I mean, you can't keep whining and shit every time shit don't go your way! I'm not ya mama or ya daddy, so I ain't gon' cater to you like they did! I'm a grown ass man, so I'ma treat you in the way that you present yourself to be treated. You wanted me to come with you to the doctor's appointment and I did. I even held your hand while she did the ultrasound and shit. You asked me to take you to get shit for the baby, I said cool. You went to try on something. I took a phone call. Simple as that. Why you gotta ask me who I was talking to? You don't pay my bill!" I said as I glanced over at her. She sat there quietly, but I could tell she was still feeling some kind of way. "I'm sorry if that hurts your feeling, but I'ma need you to grow up a little bit."

"I am grown!"

"Act like it then! You sitting there pissed off for no damn reason at all. You said you wanted to go shopping for the baby, I agreed and what'd we get? Not a fuckin' thing!" I said as she continued to pout in the seat opposite mine. She could sit there and pout until the cows came home and it wouldn't change shit until she grew the hell up.

"Wow! That's how it is, huh?"

"I'm just saying that if we're going to make this work, you need to start acting like you're 26 instead of 13. Ya feel me?"

"Yep. Sure do," she said.

The rest of the drive to her place was done in silence. When we got there, I opened the door to go inside with her, but she stopped me. "I think I'm grown enough to make it inside by myself," she said sarcastically.

"Aight, well do you then," I said as I shut my door.

She hopped out the truck and headed to her door. She unlocked the door then went inside. I backed out of the parking spot and exited the apartment complex. Sooner or later, she'd get what I was trying to say. The last thing I wanted was friction between me and Drica, but she had to stop with all that bullshit. What if I was on the phone with Keisha? What would she have done about the situation? Not a damn thing.

All she would've done was get mad the way she had just done. Women always blew things out of proportion for no reason. Now I had to go home and deal with Keisha's insecure ass. I knew that as soon as I'd walk in she'd be on her bullshit ready to ask me a million questions. All I could do was shake my head. A nigga couldn't win for shit.

The whole ride home I thought about the mess I had gotten myself into. My pops made it seem like being honest was the best way to go about things, but with a woman like Keisha, honesty wasn't an option at the moment. If I'd even attempted to mention anything to her about Drica and her pregnancy, she would really try to leave with my kids and that wouldn't end right for her. My kids meant everything to me, and I hated the fact that they were in the middle of this unfortunate situation. At the end of the day, they were the innocent ones, and that's what hurt me the most.

As soon as I got home, I was greeted with open arms by my oldest daughter.

"Daddddddddyyyyyyy!" Jalaya screamed as she ran up to me.

"What's up baby?"

I picked her up and gave her a hug and a kiss.

"I miss you dad!" She said with excitement in her voice. This little girl here looked just like her damn mama. I mean, she was like a little mini Keisha. I hated to think about when she was gon' grow up because if she was like her mama, she was gon' give niggas hell. She probably wouldn't even have no nigga in her life because that dude would have to deal with me, her, and her crazy ass mama.

"I miss you too. Where's your mommy?"

"She in the kitchen helping Aaron with his homework. She said today we get to go to Me-Maw's house."

"Is that right?" I asked with a confused look on my face.

"Yea! She said we have to go to her house so she can talk to you!"

"Whattttt?" I playfully asked. "She didn't tell me anything about that."

Jalaya nodded and gave me a kiss, then jumped down and ran into the kitchen. Confused as fuck, I followed behind her and found Keisha sitting at the kitchen table with my son. I walked around to where he was and patted him on his head.

"What up son?"

"Hey dad," he replied dryly while eyeing his mama.

That was all I needed to see to know that she had fed my kids some bullshit.

"Aye son, take your sister and go to your room for a minute. I need to have a talk with your mother."

"Okay," he said as he pushed the chair back and stood up. "Come on Jalaya."

Keisha shook her head and grabbed his arm.

"Aaron, sit down and finish your homework."

"But dad said..."

"It doesn't matter what he said," Keisha replied sternly. "Did you hear what I just said?"

He looked at me, then sat back down and picked his pencil back up.

"It's cool son. Your mom and I will go talk in the room. Come on Keisha."

She spun around in the chair and darted her eyes at me.

"I don't have anything to say to you right now."

"Keisha, I'm asking you to come and talk to me in the room. I ain't tryna do this in front of the kids."

"You might as well. They deserve the truth just like I do."

"The truth about what?" I asked.

"Dad what's wrong? Are you mad at mommy?" Jalaya asked. She's always been an inquisitive child, so why should she stop now. She took a seat at the table next to her brother and peered from me to her mom waiting for someone to say something.

"No baby. I'm not mad at her, but I think she's mad at me," I said.

"Nobody's mad honey," Keisha said. "I'm just tired of your father lying to me."

"Lying? What I lied about this time?" Keisha was always on some bullshit. She was always accusing a nigga of being dishonest, even when I was telling the truth. I mean, I know I lied today, but sometimes, I was honest about shit.

"YOU KNOW ABOUT WHAT!" She shouted as I stood up.

"Keisha, lower your voice in front of my kids, man."

"NO! THEY NEED TO KNOW WHAT'S GOING ON!"

"What's going on?" I asked irritatingly. "I don't even know what you talking about."

"I'M TALKING ABOUT DRICA AND Y'ALL BABY!"

"Bruh you still worried about that girl?"

"Who's Drica?" Aaron asked with a confused look on his face.

"Yea, who's Drica?" Jalaya asked.

"Nobody kids, she's nobody," I replied trying to diffuse the situation before shit got out of hand.

"DRICA IS YOUR FATHER'S OTHER GIRLFRIEND AND SHE'S HAVING A BABY FOR HIM!"

"What?" Aaron asked as his mouth twisted to one side. He turned to me and stared at me with disappointment in his eyes. That was the last thing I wanted to see in my kids' faces when they looked at me. I was their dad, their super hero. Keisha was wrong for fucking up the image my kids had of me. "You having a baby with another girl?"

"Who's having a baby dad? Will I have another brother or sister?" Jalaya asked.

"Nobody and no. Look, y'all need to go to your rooms. Your mother is losing it right now."

"I'M NOT LOSING SHIT!" Keisha shouted as she got in my face pointing her finger and shit. "I THOUGHT YOU SAID YOU WAS WITH LUCAS ALL DAY TODAY, HUH?"

"I was with him Keisha. What? You think I'm lying or something?"

"I KNOW YOU LYING NIGGA! CUZ LUCAS AND MAHOGANY NOT EVEN IN TOWN RIGHT NOW! YOU WOULD'VE KNOWN THAT IF YOU WOULD'VE CHECKED THEIR INSTAGRAMS BEFORE YOU DECIDED TO LIE TO ME AND USE HIM AS AN ALIBI! SO WHERE WERE YOU MARCUS? CUZ RIGHT NOW I'M STARTING TO BELIEVE THAT YOU REALLY HAVE BEEN SEEING THAT BITCH BEHIND MY BACK! I WENT TO THE CLINIC MARCUS! I WENT TO THE FUCKING CLINIC!"

"AND WHAT YOU SAW MY NIGGA?" I shouted. "HUH? DID YOU SEE ME THERE, HUH?"

"I DIDN'T SEE SHIT, BUT BITCH I KNOW YOU WERE THERE!"

"YOU DIDN'T SEE SHIT CUZ THERE WASN'T NOTHING TO SEE! KEISHA I'M TIRED OF YOU ACCUSING ME OF SHIT! LIKE REAL TALK! THIS CRAZY SHIT STARTING TO GET OUT OF HAND! LOOK AT WHAT YOU DOING IN FRONT OF OUR KIDS!" I continued to shout as they stood there in tears. "YOU GOT

THEM CRYING AND SHIT! YOU THINK THAT MAKE SENSE?!"

"BITCH YOU DON'T MAKE SENSE! ALL OF THIS IS YOUR FAULT! ALL OF IT! WERE YOU THINKING ABOUT THEM CRYING WHEN YOU DECIDED TO FUCK DRICA? WERE YOU THINKING ABOUT THEIR FEELINGS WHEN YOU CHOSE TO HAVE A BABY WITH HER? NO! CUZ ALL YOU EVER WORRY ABOUT IS YOURSELF!"

Suddenly, the baby monitor began going off. I guess all of the screaming and shouting that Keisha initiated had disturbed Kennedy.

"ALL I WORRY ABOUT IS MYSELF? YOU KNOW WHAT? I AIN'T EVEN GONNA KEEP DOING THIS WITH YOU! YOU CAN BELIEVE WHAT YOU WANNA BELIEVE, BUT THIS SHIT AIN'T GON' WORK FOR TOO MUCH LONGER! YOU NEED TO CHECK YOURSELF!"

I stormed out of the kitchen and raced upstairs to Kennedy's room, only to see her standing up in her crib screaming at the top of her lungs. I quickly picked her up and placed her on my shoulder.

"Awwwww, what's the matter with daddy baby?" I calmly asked in an attempt to soothe her. "Your mama woke you up with all of her screaming, huh?"

She continued to cry for a few more minutes, then finally quieted down. That is, until Keisha burst into the room with her noise.

"GIVE ME MY CHILD!" she yelled.

"Girl if you don't get yo' stupid ass on somewhere. Ain't nobody called you."

"GIVE ME MY CHILD MARCUS!"

"Keisha go 'head with that bullshit man. You don't think you did enough downstairs? You oughta be tryna check on Jalaya and Aaron."

"THEY'RE FINE! NOW GIVE ME MY CHILD!"

"This ain't just your child idiot. Now chill before you start her up again."

"NO YOU CHILL! GO CRADLE YOU AND DRICA'S BABY!"

Without responding, I sighed and kissed Kennedy on the cheek, then handed her to Keisha. That was the last straw.

"Yo' I'll be at my mom's until further notice."

"WHAT?!!"

"You heard me. I'm out!!"

"SO YOU JUST GON' LEAVE ME HERE WITH THREE KIDS? ALL BECAUSE YOU FUCKED UP!"

"Do you Keisha," I said as I walked out of the room.

Enough was enough. If that's how she wanted things to be, then it was what it was. I was tired of going back and forth with her about Drica. And the fact that she would get stupid the way she did in front of my kids, only made shit worse. Maybe it was time for me to draw the line and really let things go. Maybe Drica was who I belonged with. Thank God I hadn't given Keisha that ring.

CHAPTER NINETEEN

London

After crying my eyes out for the umpteenth time over Shane and his selfish antics, I finally figured out what I needed to do to get him to man up. It was going to take a lot of courage for me to do it, but I knew that would be the only way to make him understand that I was serious about everything I had said. I got my kids together and dropped them to the daycare, then plugged an address into my GPS. As I got closer to my destination, I began to get more and more nervous. But I knew that this was something I had to do.

When I got there, I pulled into the driveway and said a small prayer hoping that the outcome would be a good one. I turned off my car and unfastened my seat belt, then stepped down with a yellow envelope in my hand. I walked up to the doorstep and rang the doorbell, then stood there and patiently waited for someone to answer. I could see someone peeping through the blinds, which made me feel a little uneasy. But I was thrilled to know that someone was home. A couple of seconds later, the door cracked open. Behind it, stood a thick white woman who looked to be around my age. She had long red hair, arms full of tattoos, and dermal piercings.

"Um, I must have the wrong house," I said slowly.

Truth is, I knew I didn't have the wrong house. I just wasn't expecting her to be the one to answer the door. I mean, it was obvious that Shane fucked around with other bitches, but I was under the impression that he lived alone.

"Nah. You ain't got the wrong house," she laughed. "You and I both know that. I take it you're the girl from the voicemail. The one who said she was pregnant."

"And I guess you're the chick who called me back."

"Yep. That would be me. Were you expecting someone different?"

"Not really," I replied. "I just..."

"Yea, yea, yea. Cut the act and be real. You didn't think you'd have to answer to a white girl. I guess you thought I was some ratchet ass hoe such as yourself. But nope. I'm a snow bunny."

"Your race has nothing to do with what I assumed. But look, I didn't come here to be disrespected by some knock off Little Mermaid Ariel type bitch. Okay? I came here to have an adult conversation."

"Girl bye. A knock off I could never be. I'm the real thing baby. Something you could never be."

"Well this is the real thing too," I said as I opened the envelope and pulled out my ultrasound. "See? This is how real shit is."

"Okay and? What? You want a cookie or something? Or a round of applause?" she asked while foolishly clapping her hands. "Cuz honestly, that's all your ass will get from around here."

"No! What I want is for Shane to take accountability for his actions and take care of his child! He needs to stop dodging me and acting as if my baby will just go away because it won't!"

She cleared her throat and folded her arms, then leaned against the doorframe.

"Okay look, first of all, you're still pregnant! So it ain't shit that he could do right now! Second of all, we don't even know if that baby is really his or not! Until a DNA test is taken and he's proven to be the father, he won't be doing shit! And third, do you know how many bitches done showed up here crying wolf with the same story and trying to pin their baby on him? Countless! But guess what? Not one of those kids were his! So woman to woman, I suggest you take your lil' ultrasound and get your dusty ass off of my property! This ain't what you want sis!"

"The next bitch ain't me! So I could give a fuck about them! I know for a fact that Shane is my baby daddy, and he knows it too! So those other bitches and their false allegations don't really mean shit!" I said with an attitude. "As for as a dusty ass is concerned, maybe you should take a good look in the mirror on that one."

"And that's fine, but I said what I said so that's that! Shane ain't claiming your baby and he ain't even here right now anyway, so you need to go before I call the laws and press charges on your ass for harassment and trespassing!"

"Harassment? Bitch I didn't come here to harass you! Hell, I didn't even know your ol' ugly ass was here! And as far as trespassing, this ain't even your house! So technically you're trespassing too!"

"Actually baby girl, this is my house! But of course, you wouldn't know that, cuz you listen to everything Shane tells your green ass! One day y'all hoes will learn to stop buying dreams!"

"No bitch! Your ass will learn today!"

I pulled out my phone and immediately began dialing Shane's number.

"Who you calling hoe? The Paw Patrol?" she laughed. "Or Maury? Cuz that's the nigga you need! He would love to help you find your baby daddy and you might get famous for being on TV because you're obviously in need of some attention!"

"You'll see."

As soon as the phone started ringing, I pulled it from my ear and put it on speaker, then stood there with my hand on my hip. After four rings, Shane finally picked up.

"What you want London?"

"Shane, where are you?"

"I'm somewhere far the fuck away from you minding my damn business! Don't be calling me asking me no fucking questions about my whereabouts like you my keeper! Now what the fuck you want?"

"I'll tell you what she wants!" The girl shouted. "Her dumb ass done showed up over here with a fucking ultrasound looking for sympathy!"

"Renee?" He yelled into the phone. "Man, what the fuck kind of games y'all playing?"

"Yea bae! It's me, and I ain't playing no games! You know I don't get down like that! But this bitch came looking for you in regards to that bastard in her stomach!"

"Bitch, watch your fucking mouth!" I yelled. "Don't ever disrespect my child again!"

"Or what? Did you forget you're at MY house? I can fuck you up right now and wouldn't shit happen to me!"

"Renee, chill out!" Shane yelled through the phone. "London you ain't had no business going over there my nigga! I told you that baby ain't mine!"

"Shit I told her too!" Renee shouted again. "She don't even look like the type of bitch you'd put a baby in!"

I rolled my eyes at her and smirked.

"Shane he is yours! So you and your bitch need to stop fucking playing with me!"

"Bae, you should see her lil' ultrasound! She hopped out with her yellow envelope and everything!" Renee laughed. "She big mad!"

"Ain't nobody mad but you bitch! You can keep playing that role like you're unbothered all you want, but I bet I can say some shit that will have you second guessing your damn self!"

"Say some shit like what? Bitch you don't know me like that, so ain't shit you can say home girl!"

"Renee!" Shane shouted again. "Take yo' ass in the house and let that hoe go on about her business!"

"Oh bitch, I promise I know more about you than you think I do!"

"London shut the fuck up and move around with all that! Renee, listen to me and go in the fucking house! Quit entertaining her! I'm on my way!" Shane continued to shout.

"Nah fuck that! That bitch ain't scaring nobody! She can say what she want, but like I said, she don't fucking know me!"

"I ain't tryna scare you! I'm just tryna knock some sense into your fucking ass! You think you know your man so well, but you really don't!"

"I know he's not your baby daddy! I know he would never have me out here looking stupid like you!"

"I really feel sorry for you," I replied. "You standing up here dissing me and saying all this shit about me when you're actually in the exact same boat as me!"

"Bitch please! I could never be you! Look at me and look at you! I don't have the problems that you have, love! Unlike you, my nigga actually respects me!"

"Respect? You call this shit respect? You're dumber than I thought!"

"RENEE!" Shane yelled.

"Call it what you want, but facts are facts! Like I said, my man respects me and what we have! No matter what you try to say, he would never in a million years treat me the way he treat you hoes! Y'all let him do that shit! I don't!"

"Yea! Well, if it's like that and he respects you so much, then why the fuck did he hook up with me after your sister's birthday party in Athens?"

"Bitch what?"

"Yea! Remember when he called you from outside and told you that he had to leave for a few hours? Well I was with him! He was really leaving to go fuck me like a rabbit at the Marriott!"

"Bitch stop lying! You hoes will say anything to try to mess up a happy home! You want what I got, but it ain't happening!"

"Your home was never happy bitch! Cuz if it was, I wouldn't be standing here with your nigga baby in my stomach!"

"Girl get the fuck out of here! You're a delusional liar, and I truly feel sorry for you and that baby!"

"If you think I'm lying then ask him! You see he done got quiet!"

"Girl whatever!" I stood there with a smirk on my face while watching the sweat form on her top lip. She could pretend to be unbothered if she wanted to, but I knew what I said was having an effect on her big ass. "Shane! Is that true?"

"MAN NO! DON'T LISTEN TO THAT FUCKING GIRL! YOU ALREADY KNOW WHAT'S UP! SHE LYING! THAT'S ALL SHE DO!"

"So I'm a liar Shane? For real? You know what I'm saying is true!" I yelled.

BITTER BABY MAMA'S CLUB

"Bitch, you ain't shit but a joke!" Renee laughed. "A whole fucking clown out here! You ain't got no receipts to back up what you're saying! And before you try to say something about knowing about her party, her flyer was posted all over Instagram and Facebook for two weeks! So please miss me with the bullshit!"

"Okay! Since Shane won't tell you the truth, then I will! Didn't you text him the morning after the party asking him what time he was heading back to Decatur cuz you had a nail appointment at noon? Didn't you go off on him on Facetime cuz your sister ended up having to drop you off there and he still hadn't made it back in time to pick you up? He was in the car when you Facetimed him, right? And he rushed you off the phone right?"

She stood there listening to those words roll off of my tongue in shock. The look on her face was priceless as she began to put two and two together. She finally realized that I wasn't lying.

"Are you fucking kidding me right now?"

"No! I'm not fucking kidding you right now," I said using my white girl voice. "The joke's on you boo! Now what was it that you were saying about respect?"

"So you knew about me the whole time and still chose to fuck him?"

"He told me that he was single and that you were just somebody that he was cool with! But I didn't owe you shit anyway! So yes, technically I did know! I knew who you were the minute you came to the door earlier too! I never forget faces!"

Before she could respond, Shane pulled into the driveway next to my car and hopped out in a rage. I hadn't even realized that he had hung up. I was too busy reading this bitch and putting her dumb ass in her place.

"WHAT THE FUCK YOU DOING HERE LONDON?!"

"Nigga you know exactly what I'm doing here! Must we go through this every time I see you?"

"BITCH IF YOU DON'T GET THE FUCK OFF MY LAWN WITH YOUR DUMB SHIT! I SWEAR TO GOD!"

"You swear to God what? I told you quit playing with me! I gave you chance after chance to get your shit together, but you still wanna act stupid! So this was my last resort!"

"FUCK WHAT SHE TALKING ABOUT!" Renee shouted as she walked out of the house. "SO YOU BEEN FUCKING WITH THIS BITCH SINCE PORCHA PARTY? HUH? THIS WHAT THE FUCK YOU BEEN DOING SHANE!"

"MAN RENEE, SHUT THE FUCK UP, AND GET BACK IN THE HOUSE! I DONT KNOW WHY YOU STOOD OUT HERE AND LISTENED TO THIS HOE ANYWAY!"

"HOE?" I screamed as I walked up to him. "SO I'M A HOE NOW? I WASN'T A HOE WHEN YOU WAS ALL UP IN ME! I WASN'T A HOE WHEN YOU WAS PLANNING A FUCKING LIFE WITH ME! DON'T CALL ME OUT MY FUCKING NAME CUZ YOUR BITCH RIGHT THERE! TALK TO ME THE WAY YOU USED!"

"BITCH, YOU GOT FIVE SECONDS TO GET THE FUCK UP OUTTA HERE! ON MY MAMA!"

"OR WHAT? WHAT THE FUCK YOU GONNA DO SHANE?"

"WHAT IMA DO? YOU WANNA SEE WHAT IMA DO? HOLD ON!"

He grabbed me by the back of my neck and forcefully shoved me to the ground, then walked over me. He picked up my ultrasound and looked at it, then tore it into pieces.

"THIS YOUR LAST WARNING BITCH! STAY THE FUCK OUT MY FACE WITH THAT BULLSHIT!"

I held the bottom of my stomach and looked up at him in tears. Renee ran over to me and grabbed my arm in an attempt to help me up.

"Don't fucking touch me!" I cried out as I jerked my arm away from her.

Shane ran over to her and grabbed her arm. She turned around and punched him in his chest.

"BOY WHAT THE FUCK IS WRONG WITH YOU! DON'T PUSH THAT FUCKING GIRL!" She shouted. "I DON'T GIVE A FUCK HOW MAD YOU ARE! SHE'S PREGNANT DUMMY! YOU WANNA GO TO JAIL?"

"MAN, FUCK YOU AND HER! GET YO' FUCKING IGNORANT ASS IN THE HOUSE! YOU SHOULD'VE NEVER OPENED THE DOOR!"

"FUCK YOU! YOU SHOULD'VE NEVER DID A LOT OF SHIT! FUCKING HER IS ONE OF THEM!"

They stormed into the house and slammed the door, leaving me on the cold hard ground alone. I sat up in the grass and brushed myself off, then crawled over and picked up the torn pieces of what used to be my ultrasound off the ground. As I listened to them argue about me, I pulled myself up and slowly walked over to my car in pain. With tears rolling down my face, I opened the door and slid inside. I couldn't believe that Shane had actually went as far as putting his hands on me, but this was the last time he was going to clown me like that.

Shit, this time I swear on my mama!

CHAPTER TWENTY

Keisha

A week later...

Marcus had been gone this whole past week. I had called him countless times, but he never picked up or returned my calls. I was pissed about that because what if I was trying to reach him because one of the kids had an emergency? I hated when he acted like that. To be honest though, it had been a while since he had behaved that way. If I was to be honest once more, I missed my man. I missed talking to him. I missed hearing him tell me that he loved me. I missed him helping me with the kids and I missed making love to him.

Today was the day we were either going to make up or break up for good. I was confident that we'd make up though because I hated when we argued. Y'all know how I felt about Marcus. I loved him. I had always loved him. I'd be damn if I lost him now because of some bitch who wanted to be like me. She could never be like me because I was cute, and she was ugly, looking like a damn Troll. I know I sounded like a teenager, but Marcus had been mine since we were teens. I wasn't going to let him go that easily.

I got all the kids dressed, so now all I had to do was comb the girls' hair. I started with Jalaya first because she was the oldest and had the longest hair. She also was the one who stayed still longer. Kennedy was always moving around, but then again, she was only a year old. I didn't expect her to be able to sit still like Jalaya for a couple more years. It took me about an hour to get both of their hair done. Once I was done with that, I posted the three of them up in front of the TV and went about getting myself together.

Once I was done getting myself ready an hour later, I grabbed my kids and strapped them in the car, so we could go see their dad and grandparents. "Are you guys excited to see daddy?" I asked.

"Yaaahhhh!" They yelled happily from the back seat.

I smiled at them in the rearview mirror as I headed for their grandparent's place. I hoped that Marcus' dad wouldn't give me a hard time today because I wasn't in the mood. All I wanted to do was get my man back home to me and the kids. Half an hour later, I pulled up to the gate and pressed the numbers to dial up Ms. Lena and Mr. Raymond. I hoped that Marcus would be the one to buzz me in.

"Hello," came Mr. Raymond's voice over the intercom.

"Hey Mr. Raymond, it's Keisha!"

"Keisha? What are you doing here girl? Is Lena expecting you?"

"Uh, no. I got the kids with me and…"

"Oh, you got my babies with you?"

"Yes."

"Well, why didn't you say that first? Lemme buzz y'all in," he said. A couple of minutes later, the gate opened up, so I drove my car through. Well, there went the surprise for Marcus.

We made our way to their house and I parked the car. Marcus' dad ran outside, as well as his mother because they were happy to see the kids. They immediately opened the back door and helped the kids out of their seat belts. "Why didn't y'all tell us y'all were coming?" Ms. Lena asked.

"We were trying to surprise their dad," I said.

"Their dad? Is Marcus coming here too?" Mr. Raymond asked.

Shit, now I was confused. Why would they be asking me if Marcus was coming when he was already supposed to be here? When he left our home last week, he said he was going to stay with his parents. If he wasn't here, where was he?

"I'm confused," I said. "Hasn't Marcus been here?"

"Oh shit!" His dad said.

"Come into the house Keisha. I'm not going to discuss y'all business in front of these nosey ass neighbors of mine. Rose is like the local news spokesperson. Y'all business will be all over CNN, Fox News, and NBC by five o'clock," Ms. Lena said with a smile.

I followed them inside the house. "I'ma take the kids out in the backyard while you ladies talk," Marcus' dad said.

Once he had gone out with the kids, Ms. Lena sat down on the bar stool next to me. "So, what's going on with you and Marcus?"

"Well, we got in a huge fight last week and he stormed out. He said that he was coming here to stay with you," I explained.

"What were the two of you arguing about?"

"I don't know if I should discuss that just yet."

"Does it have anything to do with that girl that said she's pregnant for him?"

She shocked me so much I almost fell off the stool I was sitting on. How did she know about that bitch? "I heard about that. I mean, Decatur ain't that big, so mess spreads fast," she said.

"Yea, I know," I said as I nodded my head. "So, Marcus hasn't been here?"

"No honey. I haven't seen Marcus for a couple of weeks now. I've spoken to him, but I haven't seen him. Have you tried calling him?" She asked.

"Yes, but he's not accepting my phone calls or responding to my text messages."

"That's unfortunate. Well, let me check with his dad to see if he's heard from him today," she said as she slid off the bar stool and headed outside.

I tried calling Marcus again, but it just went to voicemail. I wasn't sure why he was ignoring me, but that didn't make sense. I'm his kids' mother, so he should never ignore calls from me. "Marcus, I need to talk to you. You can't keep ignoring me. We have kids together. Call me back because this shit has gone on long enough!" I said as I left a message on his voicemail.

His mom came back inside with a smile on her face. "Good news! Marcus is on his way. Raymond just buzzed him in, so he should be pulling up any minute now," she said.

"I'm gonna meet him outside. Hopefully, the two of us can have a conversation in a civilized manner."

"Please make it civilized because I don't want no shit from these neighbors."

"I promise not to act the fool in front of your neighbors," I said.

"Good. Me and Raymond will keep the kids busy while y'all talk."

I always got along with Marcus' mom even though she thought I ruined his career as well. She understood that the two of us having sex was something he and I both decided on. We both made the decision to get freaky without protection, so she didn't fault just me for what happened.

I walked over to her, kissed her on the cheek, and made my way to the front door. I opened the door as Marcus was pulling up. I guess he spotted my car because he didn't pull into the driveway. I stood there confused as hell with my arms crossed over my chest waiting for him to pull up. However, he didn't. As I walked toward the end of the driveway with my arms outstretched, he proceeded to drive away.

When the passenger's side window rolled down, and I saw the smug look on Drica's face, I almost shitted on me. What the hell was he doing with her? As she smiled at me, I could see the anger on his face as he yelled for her to raise the window. It was too late though because I had already seen what I saw.

My heart dropped as realization hit me hard in the face. All the time I had been accusing Marcus of still seeing Drica, he had denied it. He had blamed it on my insecurities and shit. But there was the truth staring me right in the face. He had been seeing her all along. As I watched his truck drive off, I sank to the ground in tears.

How could Marcus do this to us? How could he do that to our kids? He knew how important family meant to me. He knew how much I loved him and our kids. Why would he kill my dream of us getting married? Why would he ruin our happy home by messing with that homewrecker? I had loved that man more than half my life and that was the thanks I got.

As my heart smashed in tiny pieces, tears continued to fall down my face. How could I go on without Marcus? How could I do it and would the pain ever go away?

I finally got up and jumped in my car. I had to follow them. I had to find out why he played me. I sped out of the gated community unsure of where Marcus even went. I didn't have to look far though because I saw his truck parked at the convenience store right around the corner. It was parked by the front of the store, so I pulled alongside it.

I peered inside the truck and it was empty, so I got back in my car and waited for him and his bitch to come outside. I was prepared to go off on his ass because he had her get an abortion so the two of us could be together. And now he was still running around with her ass. What the fuck did she have that I didn't? What made her ugly ass so damn attractive to him?

I saw his big head making his way out of the store and I could tell that he and that heifer were having a heated conversation. They must have still been arguing. As the bitch made her way to the passenger's side door, my heart sank even further to the floor as I saw her protruding belly. I was prepared to go off on Marcus, but now, I was too stunned to do anything.

But as hurt as I was right now, this was one showdown that couldn't be avoided. I took a deep breath and stepped out of my car before the bitch could get in the truck.

"15 YEARS MARCUS! WE'VE BEEN TOGETHER FOR 15 YEARS AND THIS IS WHAT YOU DO?!" I asked shocking his ass. Drica was standing there with a smirk on her face that made me wanna slap the shit out of her. Marcus stood there with his mouth hung open as if he was too scared to say something. "DON'T' JUST STAND THERE, MOTHERFUCKER!! SAY SOMETHING!!"

"What do you want him to say? You got eyes don't you? It's staring you right in your damn face and you're still looking for an explanation?" Drica asked.

I took a deep breath because somebody really needed to get that bitch before I snatch her ass. I looked up to the sky and said, "God help me because I'm about to fuck these bitches up!"

To be continued…

Made in the USA
Monee, IL
09 October 2021

79691148R00090